How I Met My Sweetheart

A Collection of Short Inspirational Love Stories

*Anderson*Stephens-Batts*Butler*Roberts-Cargile
Fisher *Carruth-Hoffman*Hill-James
*Jernigan*McDermid**Parham
*Robinson*Smith*J. Thomas*S. Thomas
*Washington*Holt-Webb*Joe-Williams*Woodside*

[AP]

How I Met My Sweetheart
Copyright © 2007

Amani Publishing
P. O. Box 12045
Tallahassee, FL 32317
850-264-3341 Phone
850-878-1006 Fax

A company based on faith, hope, and love

Visit website: www.AmaniPublishing.net

E-mail: AmaniPublishing@aol.com

Cover Photograph: Courtesy of Istockphoto.com

ISBN: 097528519X

Library Control Number: 2006937603

Cover photo: Courtesy of Istockphoto.com

Table of Contents

Introduction

Introduction

I'm honored to begin this introduction by telling you how the concept for this book was originally conceived. It all started at a New Year's Eve party hosted by a married couple. We were all sitting around talking and having a jolly good time when the hostess turned to me and asked, "Barbara, how did you meet your husband?"

By the time I and everyone else at the party had finished answering that one question, we were all laughing. A week later, I was still laughing at some of the stories that I had heard that evening and suddenly came up with the idea for this book. After sharing my vision with a few friends, they strongly supported me in turning my idea into a publication filled with true romance stories.

Therefore, it is my strong desire that this book will be inspirational to married couples as well as singles that are still searching for love. Hopefully, through our testimonies about how we met our sweethearts, you'll be inspired to continue your quest for real intimacy.

I'm a hopeless romantic and proud of it. I've always been one and will always be one. You see, I met my sweetheart over twenty-five years ago at the age of eighteen. It feels like I've been married all of my adult life, and there's nothing else that I'd rather be.

I wholeheartedly applaud each contributor for having the courage to share a significant part of their lives with the rest of the world. I hope that you will enjoy each author's timeless love story as much as I've enjoyed publishing them.

Barbara Joe-Williams
Author and Publisher

1.

ALL THE WAY

Deborha A. Parham

Your left, your left, your left, right, left. This was the sound that was always heard on a daily basis when I entered Fort McPherson Army Post. I always seemed to be there whenever they were passing the gate.

It was there that I first saw my future husband, Wade. He was standing next to, Ray, the guy that I was currently dating. All eyes were on me as I passed their platoon. My husband used to tell Ray that he was going to take me from him, but in my mind, I never saw it happening.

Being employed on an army post, I always interacted with diverse people. I worked in Finance which meant I saw everybody that was stationed at Fort McPherson. I was always in the company of men because there were few women in my department.

I met Ray while I was walking to the credit union. It was cold outside and I was not paying him a bit of attention. However, he somehow managed to get my attention and we talked. After what seemed like hours, I agreed to give him my telephone number. He called and invited me out on a date. I told him "Yes" but really had no intention of going out. When he arrived at my apartment, I told my roommate to tell him I wasn't there. He left and when I returned to work on Monday, he had told everyone that I was 'jive.' Feeling bad, I agreed to go on a real date which led to us becoming a couple temporarily. We frequented the Non-Commissioned Officer's Club (NCO) on the weekend where my future husband, Wade, would be. He would always stare at me which made me feel so creepy.

7

As time went on, Wade's friend, Bernard, would always see me and tell me how much Wade liked me. This was interesting to me since we hardly said two words to each other except in passing. During this time, I had broken up with Ray and was not really interested in pursuing another relationship. Wade and I began to run into each other more at outings like the bowling alley and baseball games. Our conversations started to have substance.

And then he received orders that he would be going overseas for a tour of duty. He had to go to Fort Benjamin Harrison first for training before he was to ship to Korea. My friend, Sheri, and I decided to get a bunch of other friends together and have a going away picnic in the park for Wade. They all agreed and we had a wonderful time. Wade was totally surprised. We only hugged when we parted our way.

The next morning, Bernard called and told me what time Wade's flight was leaving and encouraged me to go with him to the airport to see Wade off. I did and Wade was totally surprised. To see his face as he was boarding the plane was one that I would never forget.

After his training, he went home to Petersburg, Virginia, before he shipped out to Korea. Sherri and I, along with Bernard, drove to Petersburg and surprised him. We had never met his family. They were so nice and hospitable to us. Wade and I had a very nice weekend. This would be the beginning of a beautiful relationship.

While he was away in Korea, we wrote each other almost daily. He even called me once a month from over there. My birthday was coming up and he orchestrated me a Toga birthday party with the help of my roommates and his fellow soldiers of Headquarters Company. It was nice! A call came in during the party from Korea and that's when he told me he loved me.

Soon after my party, I moved out from my roommates on my own and switched jobs. He then informed me that he would be coming home. My new job was overwhelming and I transferred back to Fort McPherson.

Wade came home and I was at the airport to greet him. It was amazing! We talked for hours. He had only been home for about one week when he asked me to marry him. I accepted and immediately he went to ask for my hand from my parents. My parents and family fell in love with him. They gave him their blessings, and my daddy even volunteered to finance the wedding. We decided on a December date; December 1, as a matter of fact. Our wedding colors were green, red, and black. Not wanting to leave anyone out, we had a wedding party of thirty-two people. It was so beautiful! Our wedding song was by Jeffrey Osborne, *We're Going All The Way.* The reception was held at an apartment clubhouse. We did not honeymoon right afterwards but had one later.

Wade's kinfolks came mostly from Washington, DC, and Virginia while most of my kinfolk came right from Atlanta, Georgia.

We renewed our vows on our 10th wedding anniversary in 1994 with our three children standing up for us. Bishop Eddie L. Long did the honors.

Wade and I have been married for twenty-two years and are still going strong. Our children are Rashi (21), a senior at Georgia Southern University; Ramoris (19), a sophomore at Georgia Southern University; and Ramaiseya (17), a senior at Middle Grove High School.

About the Author

Deborha A. Parham is a Georgia native born in Atlanta to Nathaniel Sr. and Alberta White. As a child she was involved in a car accident that left her handicapped. While incapacitated, she discovered that she enjoyed writing short stories, poems, and journaling. Thus the writer in her was born.

Her fascination with how things operated opened the door of discovery to technology. The love of technology drove her to start her own desktop publishing company, **Nite Shift Computer Services** while still working as a federal employee. The company has been in operation for 15 years. She is also co-owner of another company called **Sekret Xscapes**, which creates and prepares nights of intimacy for married couples away from home.

The title of her first book, *Beyond the Ashes*, is very dear to Deborha's heart and is symbolic of her healing process. The word, **'ashes'**, stands for *Anger, Sorrow, Hatred, Empathy,* and *Sickness*. Deborha has been a member of New Birth Missionary Baptist Church in Lithonia, Georgia, where Bishop Eddie L. Long is the senior pastor, for nineteen years.

Email: mysisterplacepub@aol.com

Website: www.deborhaparhamwrites.com

2.

ANOTHER WORLD

Kim Robinson

1991

It had been a hard night. I had worked in the penthouse up until time for me to go to the airport for my flight to Texas. I was a tour guide in Oahu, and I coordinated and hosted Luau's six nights a week.

I was also the madam of a penthouse where twenty-one call girls, which I was one of, entertained men until the early morning. I also ran an escort agency called Angels of Hawaii with an ad in the yellow pages and sold and used drugs, worked with an international credit card scam ring, and various other nefarious underworld occupations.

I had a three hour layover in Chicago. I found myself a bench and laid down and put my purse under my head and went to sleep. I felt someone looking at me and opened my eyes. A man was sitting there staring at me.

He was attractive behind the pop-bottle-bottom thick glasses and the 1970's little afro. He wore a nice designer suit, but the pants were too short showing his socks which were much too light with dark shoes.

"Hello," I said.

"You looked so peaceful," his European accent was intriguing.

I sat up and we started talking. I told him I was a tour guide going to visit a friend in Texas for a few days. What I did not tell

11

him was that the friend was in the penitentiary, and I was running drugs.

He was an engineer traveling from Texas to Washington on business. He had recently relocated to Texas with his job and was separated from his wife.

We talked until I had to board my flight.

He telephoned a few times over the next few months and talking to him was like a breath of fresh air. Then he called and told me he was coming to Hawaii on business. He said that he would arrive on Monday and be done with his business meetings by Wednesday evening.

I arranged for two of my employees to take over for me from Wednesday to Friday when he was going back home. I checked into a hotel on the Big Island where I was not so well known. I hoped that I would not run into anyone who knew me.

He was so different from everyone else in my life. He was square and untainted and I felt like I was Cinderella, pretending to be someone else until the clock struck twelve, only instead of a few hours, my carriage was now scheduled for a few days. We hit all the tourist attractions on the Island, something that with my busy schedule, I had not been able to do in the three years that I had been in Oahu. We went to wineries, coffee, and pineapple plantations.

We went to a luau that night, and for the first time, I was not working and could relax and enjoy myself. We walked along the beach and swam in the moonlight. We curled up in a lounge chair on the beach and talked about our childhoods until we both fell asleep. I never slept around a client, but he was not a client and I felt safe around him. .

We were awakened by the beach boys coming out to set up. We went to my room and neither of us wanted him to go to their own room. I invited him in and we curled into one another and slept. I slept like I had not slept in eleven years. No beepers, no phones, and no work. Just a peaceful sleep spooned into him.

I woke to a knock on the door, and I jumped up in alarm to the unfamiliar surroundings. My heart slowed when he walked in from the balcony. He must have seen the look on my face because he said, "Relax, I ordered breakfast."

We ate on the balcony and planned our day. We visited museums and went to the top of a dormant volcano. We took in dinner and a show with a friend of his who lived on the island.

I knew who the guy was, but he did not know me. He was a frequent client of the Escort service. He kept asking me if we had met. Something about my voice was familiar to him. It should have been; I had been sending him girls twice a week for the last two years.

I changed my voice a bit, and luckily, he never made the connection. After the show, we went back to the club in our hotel. Before going up, he asked me to stay in his room. I went to my own room and showered and changed and went to his room. We slept as we had the night before. This was going to be our last night together. When I woke in the morning, I watched him sleep. Something that had been dormant in me since I had had my heart broken eleven years earlier woke, and I wanted to be with him. His eyes opened, and he must have seen the desire. We spent the morning making love until I fell asleep.

I woke and he was on the phone, it was business. I sat on his lap and soon he was off the phone and we went back to bed. When I woke again, he was back on the phone. There were only a couple of hours left before his flight. I got up and gathered my things. I did not want to deal with any goodbyes. I would gather my things and slip out the door. It was over and I felt as if I was going to cry when I thought about the life I was going back to.

As I walked toward the door he hung up the phone, "Where are you going?"

"Well, you have to get ready to go, and I see you have business, I was going to get out of your way."

He walked over and took my purse from me and pulled me to the bed. "If I stayed until Sunday, would you stay with me?"

My heart soared and I almost jumped up and flew around the room. "I think it could be arranged," I said with a big smile on my face.

"Good because I already changed my flight. Let's get dressed and move you to my room. No sense having two rooms." After we dressed, we went down to the desk where he paid for my room and checked me out. We took my things to his room.

13

We had a late lunch and rented a moped and rode along the roads, and picnicked on the beach. We spent our last two days in the room and on the beach around the hotel.

I woke early Sunday morning and watched him sleep. I knew my carriage would soon turn back into a pumpkin. My heart hurt. I took some of the hotel stationery and wrote a poem:

Being In Love and Making Love

When you can take a simple kiss
Generate it through a person's soul
It's impossible to compare this
Except to say it makes me whole

The knowledge that I have been deprived
No longer ignorant to my body's needs
A beautiful yet brutal awakening
A birth, to a new aspect of my life
Bringing to focus a natural greed

The daily unfolding of my flower
Giving more feeling than I can afford
Only one person can execute this power
Prayers of endurance I send to the Lord

Being in my only true lover's arms
A safe place, a shelter, a haven
A place where there can come no harm
Making me, the most cowardly woman brazen

Tender moments, thoughts of shared events
A look of kindness, a hand brushed over
A wrap of warmth to sleep in slumber
Erasure of memories and nights of torment
Feeling a goodness under which I can hover
Some of life's terrors have been encumbered

Never discouraging, full of daily encouragement,
Knowledge of faith lighting up the way
Depleting disparagement
Every achievement like a brand new day
I love the time we spent together

Kim

I took the poem and folded it and put it in an envelope that I sprayed with my perfume. I took out his planner that I had seen him writing appointments in, and I turned the page to two days ahead and put the envelope there.

Our flights were within fifteen minutes of one another. He bought me a book at the airport store and gave it to me. When I got on the plane I opened the book and an envelope fell out of it. When I opened it, there was a check.

For a moment I feared that somehow he knew what I was. I read the letter and my fears were assuaged.

"Kim, I know that you had to pay others to take over at work for you, and I did not want you to lose anything. I put this in here because I know you probably would not have taken it. I had a wonderful time and look forward to seeing you again."

Ten years later, we had endured a lot of drama, but we stayed together. We married on a beach in Negril, Jamaica, surrounded by family and friends. Our six-year-old son was the ring bearer; he looked so handsome in a tux that matched his father's. Our five-year-old daughter was my flower girl wearing a dress that matched mine. I am saved now and a proud PTA mom. Boy, if my old partners in crime could see me now.

<u>About the Author</u>

Kim Robinson resides in Dallas, Texas. She is the author of *Roux in the Gumbo*, and two virtual cookbooks. Currently, she's writing a story entitled *Street Life to Housewife*, a title which speaks for itself. She has four other books near completion. One is best described as Murder, She Wrote 'for the hood.' G-mama is a sixty-eight-year-old, ex gang banger/ex hustler, who sits in her rocking chair solving crimes that cross her porch. She believes that, "the penitentiary ain't nothing but college for criminals," and there is a way to do penance for your crimes that will make things right in God's eyes. Her goal is an eight book series.

She is close to completion on *God Ain't Spelled Government*. Alumni of Dominguez High School, Class of 77' has leaked a government conspiracy at her twenty year class reunion. The government does not know who she leaked to, so they set out to kill everyone who attended the reunion.

E-mail: Kim@KimRobinson.com

Website: www.Kim-Robinson.com

3.

BITTERSWEET

Luvenia M. Hill-James

How I met my husband is somewhat bittersweet. When I met him, a man was the absolute farthest thing from my mind. When I say, "The farthest thing from my mind," I really mean the farthest thing. I really, really mean the farthest thing from my mind.

I had been in a relationship and my heart had been broken into a trillion pieces, but I must give God honor because He healed me from the relationship; not only did God heal me from the worn out relationship, God healed me of so many other things as well. God delivered me from having to work two jobs and never getting enough rest, raising my children as if I was the first and only single parent in this great big world.

Over a course of time, I began to see myself as a piece of glass that had been shattered by many different things in life, things that affected me personally. I never saw myself as a "pretty girl" and often heard others call me "big eyes" and "dark" in a negative way.

Later on in life, I watched my dad fade away with sickness and soon after my heart suffered another chipping. The best brother, in my opinion, broke me down. My brother committed suicide. I wanted to die with him. He cheated us, his family, his wife and children and grandchildren, his nieces and nephews out of knowing him, an opportunity to reap from his wisdom and so much more.

It is said that good friends are far and few in between. I am glad to say that I had a very, very good friend. As a matter of fact, she was my best friend. She was the sweetest friend a young lady could have. No matter what I did or was contemplating, she was always in my corner. She was not too critical of my mistakes, but she was definitely critical as a friend could be. My friend gave me room to make mistakes even after she expressed she did not believe some of my decisions to be a good idea. She said to me that her mama always told her the best kind of lesson is a bought lesson. Along the way, I learned that life's lesson would prove to be very expensive.

This friend of mine talked about God and Jesus and the power of the Holy Spirit a lot. She often said that I should stay anchored in my faith and belief in God. Let nothing move or shake me from it. My friend would often say to me that, "God will never leave you, nor will He forsake you. He (God) will stick closer to you than a brother. He will be a father for the fatherless and a mother for the motherless." Throughout her conversation she would often quote Scriptures and share the advice of her grandmother and mom. She really was a good friend to me. The best life has to offer.

During some of our conversations, she would say to me that I am going to introduce you to your husband. I would reply, "I have my husband." I was talking about my relationship with Jesus the Christ and I did not want anybody to interfere or try to come between us. You see, Jesus and I had a thing going on. He treated me really wonderfully, better than I had ever been treated in my life. He was good to me.

I did not mention to you that for many years my friend had been sick. She had strokes, yes, more than one; she had heart attacks, yes, more than one. She even began to have amputations, but she still had hope and most importantly, she maintained joy.

By now I am sure you are wondering, what does this have to do with meeting my husband and how? Patience is a virtue. I must tell you who my best friend is. I won't give her name, but I will tell you this much about her: She was a woman of her word. She often went overboard to keep her word to me and to all of her children. My best friend was my mother. A (Proverbs

31) woman, strong and courageous, believing nothing was too hard for her with the help of God. And I did rise up and call her blessed.

Throughout her life she tried to teach her children the same philosophy but when we come of age, and reach a certain point in our lives we begin to believe what we want. Mama never stopped loving us in spite of it all. She never gave up on us. No, not ever.

Even to this day I remember the strong, independent woman of medium stature, the blackest hair I have ever seen, a coffee completion, round face, pearl eyes, full lips and a smile that would wrap around this world. Mama had the perfect arms, they were perfect because she always had a hug for her children and never missed a moment to say, "I love you."

Then it happened. She began to get sick, but over the years I saw a fighter. A woman who refused to leave her children until she knew our faith in God was stronger than our love for her. She had been sick for a while and I believe she knew better than the doctors, her family and friends, that her time to leave this world was drawing near.

My mama began to tell me to go out go to a restaurant, go to a movie, or even church, meet someone, and begin to date. Take some time for yourself. When I leave this world, "I need to know that you are going to be okay."

For the first time in my life, I did not want to hear her advice. I did not want to hear what she had to say. For one reason, I was tired. I was working two jobs to make ends meet. I personally felt like I did not have time to deal with anyone else other then me, my mom, and my children. Another reason was that I was dealing with three hardheaded children, (two daughters and a son who are the best children in this world and to me, they are truly gifts from God).

I had prayed and asked God to bring me back into one piece, put me back together again and make me whole. As shattered as I was, I was not completely broken. There was something holding me together. THERE HAD TO BE.

My mother got sick for the last time, and the story is as follows:

I got up early on March 11th, a Monday morning, and headed into work. As I put my foot out of the door, I heard in my spirit, in the gut of my stomach into my ears, "Go back, go back and kiss your mother."

I obeyed the voice and went back. I kissed her and said to her, "I love you" and she said "I love you" and this went on for a little while. Finally I said to her, "You just don't know how much I love you," and she said to me, "I believe I do." I then said to her, "I am coming home early to spend some time with you. We can go riding or do whatever you want to do."

That day she was taken by ambulance to the emergency room, but by the time I arrived she was in a coma, never to come out again. For the next twenty days I stayed at the hospital with my friend, my mom, my mother.

For several days, the doctors gave us hope but shortly after that, they began to tell us that she was having mini strokes back to back and would not come out of it.

By faith, I begin to pray and talk with God, but it was His will.

Around day ten or eleven, I said to her, "You have never broken your promises or not kept your word. You said that you were going to introduce me to my husband and if you die, mama, you will have lied to me. So you can't die until you meet my husband. I need to know that all is well with you. I need to know that you will be okay with him, that he is the kind of guy that you can call your son."

My mother was taken from critical cardiac care into the Intensive Care Unit. I walked past an extremely tall figure, but that's all it was, a figure. I did not want her to leave me.

Again, once we were in ICU, I expressed to her, softly in her ear, "You can't leave me until I know you will be okay with my husband." Suddenly, one of the machines goes off and begins to beep, beep in her room and the tall figure walked in again. He smiled and said hello.

Me, I was hurting. Hurting really badly and to be honest, I don't even remember speaking or acknowledging his presence. I pulled my Bible out and began to read, and in between reading to her I would remind her of her promise to introduce me to my husband. It always seemed as if something would go wrong in her room and he would have to come in.

Finally, it came to a point where he noticed I had not been eating. He would order trays for me and inquire if I was okay.

How could I be okay when the life channel I came into this world through was leaving through another channel? *No, I am not okay,* is what I was screaming in my silence. *Stop asking.* But he didn't.

It was not long before he was more than a figure that I had not put form to. He continued to speak and be concerned about my health. One day he said to me, "I don't know your mom, but I don't think she would want you to starve yourself." I looked up at him in anger and depression and for the first time I saw his smile was big but soft. This giant of a person, he was over six feet tall, soon became my sounding board.

He continued to be kind to me and suggest I eat when it was sent in, but I wouldn't. I was not looking or being looked for at this time. My hair was in two braids and I wore big shirts, jeans, and sneakers daily while I was at the hospital. I did not recognize myself.

Every morning between 5:30 and 6:30, I had to leave ICU. I went to my daughter's apartment to shower and return to the hospital and stayed there with my mom around the clock. I could not stand to see the 5:30 - 6:30 hour because I had to leave her room and pray that she would be alive when I returned, and then the day came when we had to remove my mom from the ventilator. He stayed in the room, along with some others until we said that we wanted to be alone with her.

He went home, but he called back and asked the night nurse to make sure I was comfortable, to make sure I had a chair and blanket to cover my shoulders, while I lay my head on the bed next to my mother.

He called throughout the night and finally I said to my mother, "You said to me that you would introduce me to my husband, but you won't open your eyes. You won't respond to me. The only person that I have met or that has come in your room, mama, is the male nurse. You have to introduce me to my husband." Then the phone rang. It was him, the figure of a person I'd come to know. He called to see if I was okay, if I needed anything. I looked over at my mom and it appeared to me that there was a smile on her face and her machine beeped for the very last time.

I am a true believer that God will not take something from your life without replacing something in your life. My mom was comfortable enough to leave at that moment, and I was comfortable enough believing that she kept her word until the very last second of life.

Gary, the male nurse, and I went to a small restaurant that is closed now. He was trying to get me to eat. So I will call this our first date. Otherwise, he held my hand at my mother's funeral, and he assisted in carrying her to her final resting place.

You can say we became best friends. He took care of my loving mother, now I am in his loving care.

The last Scripture I read to mother is Psalm 23:
> The Lord is my shepherd, I shall not want.
> He maketh me to lie down in green pastures;
> He leadeth me beside the still waters.
> He restoreth my soul;
> He leadeth me in the paths of righteousness for his name's sake.
> Yea though I walk through the valley of the shadow of death, I will fear no evil; For thou art with me;
> Thy rod and thy staff they comfort me.
> Thou preparest a table before me in the presence of mine enemies;
> Thou anointest my head with oil; my cup runneth over.
> Surely goodness and mercy shall follow me all the days of my life; and I will dwell in the house of the Lord forever.

I shared my mother's favorite Scripture for this reason:
God will not shut a door (Mom leaving this world) without opening a window (my husband). We were married August 2, 2003. This is how I met my sweetheart. It was at the end of one chapter and the beginning of another chapter in my life. Now that's truly bittersweet.

<u>About the Author</u>

Luvenia M. Hill-James was born in Monticello, Florida. Throughout her life she has called herself a loyalist. She is a loyalist to her family, friends, and even her career. She is a dedicated wife, mother, and grandmother. She's also a hard worker and a believer in family and in the Almighty God. Luvenia is married to Gary, and they currently reside in Tallahassee, Florida, with their three children: Al'Tia, Brooke, and Freddie. They also have five beautiful granddaughters.

She is a certified Crime Intelligence Analyst who has been employed with the same State of Florida agency since November 1981. She states, "Family and friends are very important to me. I have learned over the past years just how much I love the Lord and how much deeper my love grows from day to day."

Email: gjjay357@aol.com

4.

ELEVEN

Lance Washington

It was the perfect setting. A romance filled atmosphere with candlelight, flowers, and music. Yes, our meeting was at a wedding. "I want to introduce you to someone," is the phrase we both heard from our soon to be married friends. I was a groomsman and she, Lynel, was a bridesmaid. During the reception, the bride and groom found a way to take time from all their wedded bliss to put their plan of our meeting into action. So began the introductions. The conversation went well and numbers were exchanged. A little conversation and a little dancing. A great backdrop for the start of a possible relationship.

At the time, we were both in college. Our focus was on our studies. We talked constantly about our futures; where we wanted to go and where we saw ourselves in a few years. Many of our goals were in sync with each other. It was no surprise that we became best friends. However, I liked her more than that. I wanted more than friendship. I wanted her to be with me and me only. There was only one problem with this plan, she wasn't interested in me. What could I do to change her mind? Was there anything I could do? Not really. She was set on keeping our relationship a friendly one, but I wanted more. Broken up by this, I did the only thing I thought I could do: accept being best friends.

As time went on, she would introduce me to a couple of her friends not knowing that I had no intentions of becoming interested in them. Sure her friends were cool and good company, but she was the one I wanted. Nevertheless, I went out with them. One of them caught the interest of one of my friends. So I did what any guy would do, step aside. She, however, wanted to be with me, but that was a no go. I just wasn't having it. I encouraged my friend to make his advances on this young lady and it finally worked. I was free from the setup. Or so I thought.

Enter the second friend. One more obstacle to overcome in my quest to one day be at my own wedding with the friend I met at a wedding. Well, another date and a good time as well. Yes, the second friend seemed to work out better than the first; things were good. But a strange thing started to happen. We started double dating. Yes, with the girl I still wanted in my future. Now I became more determined to be with her, I went out on these "double dates." And I have to admit, I hated it. Every second of it. She was holding hands with this other guy she liked. Well, I guess she thought she liked him, but they were not a perfect fit. She would never know I thought that. If she did, she would hate me. "Why are you trying to break us up?" she would probably say. I kept my mouth shut. I just couldn't fathom speaking those words. I wanted to tell her "He's no good for you. You're my perfect fit." But I moved on with date number two. No connection there either. She called it off and I was in total agreement.

The friendship continued on for a few years, and I'm not sure how or when it happened, but she told me that she might have feelings for me. That's right, ME. The one she didn't have any interest in at the start. FINALLY! But her timing couldn't be worse. Now I had a girlfriend, someone with whom I truly had developed a strong bond. This time the feelings were mutual. We would go on to play the game of relationship tag, when she had someone I didn't, and vice versa. We kept in touch as friends during each other's relationships. Each wanting the other, but respecting each other's commitments.

As time went on, our friendship grew stronger, relationships started and ended opposite one another, and our feelings for each other were cast aside out of respect. The next event would be one that would change everything. I would move away to advance my career. The phone calls were not as frequent. After some time, there was no communication. Although I tried to make a long distance relationship work with my current girlfriend, she would soon leave me. I remained single for a few months, not

25

really trying to find or thinking about a love connection. But one day, as thoughts of friends went through my mind, she came up. The one with whom I never had a relationship. Friends forever, but now out of touch. That day as my thoughts dwelled on long lost friends, my fingers started to dial a once familiar number hoping to hear her voice and not a recording.

"…Hello?" Lynel said.

"Hello there, stranger! What's up?"

The friendly connection that was lost was now found again, just miles apart. We talked for a short time and traded email addresses. Ah, that wonderful friendship that I left behind was now at the forefront of my mind. Of course, the question came up:

"So who are you dating?"

She would answer, "No one right now," and I the same. Yes! The stars were aligned for us to expand our friendship to another level. Emails would turn into phone calls and phone calls would turn into sky high long distance bills.

Then, out of the blue, I came up with a novel idea.

"Why don't you come visit me?" I asked, and the answer was a resounding, "When!?!"

The arrangements were made; the date was set for the visit of a lifetime. Was this finally it? Would we decide to be exclusive to each other? Would our years of friendship go to the next level? All the questions we had would be answered the second day of the visit.

"Should we explore being exclusive with one another?" I asked.

She simply replied, "Yes."

So now things had come full circle. Happiness was found and things progressed.

The courtship went on for a couple of years, leading to the reality that we were soul mates. The culmination for us was wedded bliss. And as irony plays its part and as fate would have it, we were married on the exact day and the exact month we met, ELEVEN YEARS LATER.

<u>About the Author</u>

Lance Washington is a two time regional Emmy award winning photojournalist. He writes short stories during his free time and hopes to write short stories and publish them at a later time. Lance attended Delgado Community College and the University of New Orleans where he majored in Television Production.

He resides in New Orleans, Louisiana, with his wife, Lynel, and their twin sons. She is a freelance book editor who may be reached at <u>LMaria23@hotmail.com</u>.

Email: <u>LKWashington1@yahoo.com</u>

5.

IN THE BEGINNING

Alesica Smith

In the beginning God created a man and a woman, and that woman being my aunt, who lived in a small town, Choctaw, Alabama. Within this union, they created a son, with the end result being that their love slowly drifted away after the birth of their son and they parted only to find love and each other again. This time they were in Cleveland, Ohio. By then, my aunt had already had three other children from a relationship during their time apart. Together again, they found everlasting love and two more beautiful children.

This is where our story begins, and where all the love between my sweetheart and I began. We continued a generation of love to a level that could make family and love survive and conquer all things. You see, his uncle and my aunt began a family history of love long before he and I were thought of.

The year was 1978. My sweetheart and I were five and six, respectively. We were playing in his backyard, only a house away from our aunt and uncle's. From that day on, I would never forget the most noticeable lime green houses in my life! They hold a piece of memory in them.

My sweetheart and I share everything from family to hearts. We would see each other a lot as we grew up. At one point, when we became teenagers, we started to explore the big things you think are important when you are venturing out into young adulthood and didn't see each other at all. There was a time when we were sixteen and seventeen-years-old, we would converse over the phone only to find we didn't have the same interests.

Somehow I never stopped thinking about him, even when I met my two girls' dad. I would ask our cousin about him, and she would tell me he had been asking about me too! I would never tell her to give him my number since I was in a relationship with my girls' dad. I truly believed in being faithful to the man that I was with.

I was with this man for six years, since I was sixteen years old. We split when my youngest daughter was almost a year old. At the time, he took a part of me that I thought I would never get back. I thought I would never trust another man again. I knew that this man had no love for me when we argued in front of our kids on a summer night at his mother's house. The end resulted with him putting a loaded gun in my mouth after beating me up. I can remember him begging me to say that he wouldn't pull the trigger. At this moment, I can't say that I was scared for my life, but for my children's. The only thing I could think to do was to say that I was sorry and hope that I would still be in one piece.

After that incident, I had vowed to myself that I didn't need him in our life anymore, and I loved myself too much to get back with a man like that no matter how sorry he was. I struggled for a time with mental issues. I suffered from Post Traumatic Stress Disorder and started to see a counselor for it. I had come to a conclusion while sitting in her office one day. I realized I didn't need a psychologist whose life probably was worse than mine telling me how to survive through this ordeal. That day, I simply left her office never to return again.

At the age of twenty-two, I was a single mom on welfare, but I gathered my mind together, and I weathered a storm. I had created a bubble around myself, sheltered by the great man above. I prayed and read my Bible every night. I wanted my world to work and slowly things started to change in my life one after the other. I got off of welfare, I had a working vehicle, and I started building a whole new world for myself and my kids.

After being solo for four years, I found my first love all over again! It took this long for us to realize that what was in the beginning would be until the end. I can say that he and I had met all over again with lots of love at a family picnic at my aunt's house. It was one of the green houses that I will always have treasured memories of.

He was in the process of ending his relationship with his kids' mother when I came into the picture. I guess you can say that they had the type of relationship that was on the burning ends. That day at the picnic, I think that he really liked what he saw.

One particular night, my cousin and I were going to her friend's party, and I didn't know that he would be there. I was sitting in a chair when he came up to me and gave me a kiss on the cheek and left. From then on, whenever he would see me, he would always give me a kiss on the cheek.

But this particular day, he came over to our cousin's house, and he gave me a kiss on the lips. From then on, her house became our meeting place. It was a place we could be comfortable and still enjoy our shared family. One day, his daughter and my daughter predicted that we were going to be together. I mean really be together and they were comfortable with that idea. I think that's what really made both of us more settled and comfortable about being together.

Here we are today with a love that goes deeper than skin that began with our kin folks. At one point when I was younger, I thought maybe it was a nasty thing to like my cousin's cousin since she was also his cousin. My mother told me it was okay because we weren't related by blood. Now I know we have something together that runs in between blood and family.

Although sometimes we have our disagreements, I am glad that I was strong enough to let myself love again because my sweetheart takes care of home and happiness here.

<u>About the Author</u>

Alesica Smith is a thirty-three-year-old mother of three who resides in Cleveland, Ohio, along with her future husband. Hopefully, one day, when they are financially comfortable, they'll get married after seven years of devoted love and dedicated heart-to-heart, one-on-one love.

She hopes to bring a fresh new face to the writer's scene. She is currently a teacher in the early childhood education field. Miss Smith enjoys spending her spare time with her children, reading, writing, and drawing. Alesica plans to publish her original book of poetry titled, *Treasures in Poetry,* later on this year.

E-mail: Mizzluvlea07@oh.rr.com

6.

JET and REV

Juanita E. Thomas

The Background

Once upon a time, back in the day, BSU stood for Baptist Student Union. It was a social gathering for college and ministerial students. The local churches, mainly Baptist, sponsored a weekly meeting, fellowship, and recreation time for the students. On Saturday evenings at the BSU Headquarters, young people from five or six institutions of higher education in Nashville, Tennessee, came together to discuss the Sunday School lesson, eat, talk, and get to know each other. Each year in the spring, a day and a half conference was held with some of the best known Christian Educational leaders of the city. This event took place on the North side of town at Vanderbilt University. That's where the magic happened.

The Meeting

I had been very active on my campus at Tennessee State University (TSU), and was president of the campus chapter at this time. On Saturday mornings, students would come from all over, even from the American Baptist Theological Seminary (ABT). Men and women were studying to be preachers, missionaries, and Christian educational workers.

The day session ended about three o'clock p.m. I was riding the bus like most of the students in those days. There standing at the bus stop was this tall, dark, and handsome man that had attended the conference.

He asked, "Which bus do I take to get across town to ABT Seminary?"

I told him, of course. We would take the same bus downtown, and then transfer to different buses. "I think you take the East Nashville or Bordeaux Bus."

The first bus came. We boarded.

He politely asked, "May I sit with you?"

I quickly said, "Yes!"

Thus the conversation started. It wasn't just small talk either. He said right off, "I've been watching you at the center. You come every Saturday night." He went on to say, "You really seem to have things under control. You have a way with people and seem to enjoy what you do."

When finally, I was able to get a word in edge wise, I said, "I remember seeing you too. You are not from around here are you? Where are you from?"

Spencer told me, "I'm from Seattle, Washington. Have you ever been to the west coast?"

"No!" As I thought to myself, *that's the end of the world.*

All too soon we were in downtown Nashville and had to transfer to different buses. His parting words were, "May I call you sometime, Juanita?"

"Yes, Spencer," I said giving him my phone number.

I caught the Herman Street Bus and that seemed to be a long bus ride. The bus was crowded and people were standing up. That didn't bother me as I kept thinking about the first bus ride and who sat next to me. I wondered if he would call. What would I say? Would he ask me out? What would I say?

The Date

Spencer called the next day, which was Sunday, and asked to come by my house after church. He borrowed a friend's car and came by. My mother fell in love with him at first sight (I think I did too). As

I said, he was tall, dark, had Bible knowledge, and a sharp memory for historical events and dates, particularly Black History.

Yes, the young man from far away places 'came-a-calling' on that Sunday evening as he said he would. It was in the fall of the year, as I recall; colleges and universities had been in session about six weeks. Four o'clock in the afternoon, Spencer rang the door bell and my heart skipped a beat. By this time, we had both changed from our 'church clothes' into something casual. I remember well his wearing tan slacks, a brown small plaid sports coat, and a skinny string tie. My guess is, he didn't remember what I had on, neither did I. But once again, he made an impression on me!

I think I said, "Come in." Then we sat and talked for a few minutes.

He asked "Would you like to go for a ride?"

My reply was, "Where will we go?"

"Where would you like to go?" he continued.

Remember this was the 50's in the south. There were not a lot of options for college students, not much time either. Most of the kids I knew worked, went to school, and studied. A real date consisted of a movie or maybe a ride through the park and checking out Jefferson Street. I suggested we drive through Hadley Park, look at the beautiful homes, and see what was happening in the neighborhood.

We did just that; spent about an hour then it was time to head back; since we both had to study and prepare for the next day. It was a short date, but it was the first of many to come.

What more can I say? The next thing I knew, Spencer was invited to Sunday dinner. I lived at home during my four years of college. Times were hard then. This friendship turned into a steady one which led to a wedding proposal. I was in my senior year at TSU and told Spencer to wait until after graduation for my answer, which was just a few months away. My answer produced a graduation present of an engagement ring.

I'm a widow now with precious memories; forty-two years with the same sweetheart I met that day at the bus stop.

<u>About the Author</u>

Mrs. Thomas is a retired educator. She is a widow, mother of two adult daughters and two deceased children, a sister, auntie, a friend, a Christian, and church member. She was born and educated in Nashville, Tennessee and lived in, Seattle, Washington, for over forty years, and now resides in Tallahassee, Florida.

Mrs. Thomas is an author, encourager, speaker, and teacher. She has written and published three books and is working on the fourth. *Marcia: A Celebration of Life,* is a loving family story about the battle of their middle daughter with Sickle Cell Anemia. Her second publication, *Just a Thought,* is a collection of poems, meditations, and inspirational passages perfect for daily reflections. And, similar to her first two publications, *Backside of the Pulpit,* is an insightful and spirit filled account of life as a minister's wife and the devoted supportive role of the family.

Currently, she's promoting her fourth published book titled, *On Second Thought.* Mrs. Thomas is available for church functions, women's activities, speaking engagements, seminars, and workshops.

E-mail: Jetflo5@peoplepc.com

7.

JUST FOR ME

Aleigha A. Butler

My sweetheart and I met accidentally in November 1995. My girlfriend, Darlene, said, "Girl, you know my twin sister is getting married next week."

I replied, "I love weddings. I should go home with you."

She exclaimed, "That'll be great! You'll get to meet my family, my twin, and we'll just have a good time."

"You don't think that she'll mind?" I inquired. "I don't want to be a stranger inviting myself to someone's wedding."

Darlene said, "Nonsense girl, I am going to call my parents and tell them that I'm bringing you home with me. We won't have to worry about a place to stay. We're staying with them."

We had become good friends since we met through ex-boyfriends that were best friends.

The weekend had arrived. We drove from Atlanta down I-20 East through a very tree-filled scene the entire way there. As we crossed the state line, we saw little shops, a sign that read "The Home of James Brown" and other scenery that indicated that we were in small towns and townships of South Carolina. Once we had gotten there, Darlene said, "It's not much longer."

We arrived in Hampton, South Carolina. As a Carolina girl, I was used to small towns, but I had never heard of this city. I'm from Gaffney.

We drove threw the downtown area where there were shops and the old time cinema that had one film showing. It appeared to have been closed down. This town had watermelons on all kinds of signs and displays. This was the town of the Watermelon Festival.

36

People from miles around would come to this town just to join the festivities, watch the parade, and all of the other things that it had to offer. Hampton had just opened its first McDonald's restaurant. It was evident that there was no mall, just grocery stores, dollar stores, and local chains that had been in existence for many, many years.

The church was located in the center of town (near the new McDonalds). Huspah was an older established church. Its brick exterior was well kept despite its age. As we walked in, it was as though all eyes stopped, all voices got quiet, and everyone was focused on us. First of all, Darlene modeled, so she was used to that type of reaction. I, however, was not used to it.

I walked down the short aisle of the wooden pews. Darlene went up to her twin, Arlene (the bride-to-be), and hugged her. She immediately introduced me as her friend.

It appeared that the rehearsal had already begun. Once all of that was established and I was introduced, everything resumed. The bridesmaids went to the back of the church where they originally were waiting on their queue to enter. I didn't see the groomsmen at all. I imagined that they would come out at some point.

Darlene told me that her cousin wanted to meet me. I really wasn't interested in meeting anyone, especially a man. I had just turned twenty-one-years-old, but had lived a Jerry Springer episode in my love life already. I was only interested in coming to the wedding and enjoying the scenery.

She said, "My cousin, Dexter, wanted me to tell you 'Hi,' but his ex-girlfriend is here too. It was a recent break-up so he didn't want to start a scene."

At that point, I knew that I didn't want to know him, meet him, or anything else. I wanted no dealings with this man. For this reason, I replied, "Tell him that I said 'Hello,' but I am not interested in coming here to do anything but attend a wedding. The fact that his ex-girlfriend is here is all the more reason I want nothing to do with him. Again, tell him 'Hello,' but I didn't come here to have to fight anyone that I don't know over a man I don't know and have no interest in knowing."

37

Besides, I was planning to just focus on my career. Neither did I want or need more drama in my life. I had had just about enough of the male species right then. I just wanted to turn my focus on things that I wanted to do, like traveling and simply enjoying life.

They went through the processional several times until it was perfect. The rehearsal was finally over.

At the rehearsal dinner, Dexter said 'Hello,' and I said 'Hello' back, and that was all I planned to say. I thought that this chocolate brother was handsome, but I had no desire for a long distance relationship. Although I had never met him before, there was something familiar about him. He reminded me of my grandfather. He had a perfect complexion and flawless skin. He was definitely someone that I would want to get to know better under different circumstances.

Once I discovered that he was a police officer, I really wanted to rule him out because he worked in a dangerous profession. Let's face it; police officers serve in a capacity that requires them to risk their lives everyday, and I just didn't want to have to deal with that either. I was too young for "the drama."

The wedding was simply beautiful. Arlene was a beautiful bride. Dexter had to leave early from the reception to go to work. He told Darlene to tell me that he was going to drop by her parents' house, where we were staying, later. Of course, I was clearly uninterested in hearing that. I just wanted to come to the wedding, visit my friend's family, and go back home. I kept reminding her of my reason for being there.

As he said, Dexter came to Darlene's parents' house later that evening. He was in uniform, and man did this brother look nice. I tried to continue to act uninterested and shy, but it didn't quite work. He left his patrol car running so I figured that he wasn't staying long.

I had never been attracted to a man in a uniform, but this brother was simply perfect in every sense. His broad shoulders stood out more in this shirt. I thought he was handsome in the tuxedo at the wedding (although I pretended not to notice), but he had me speechless at the sight of him now.

The conversation that I thought would only take a few minutes turned into an hour. We talked about everything from our interests to what we did currently to what we were interested in for the future. He also mentioned that he desired to live in Atlanta one day.

Being a pessimist, I figured he was just feeding me some lines. I had seen it all so many times before. You meet this perfect guy, date several years, he takes your heart, and then he's gone. I wasn't letting this man get close to me. I looked at the clock again, and another hour had gone by. We were talking as if we had known each other for years. There were so many things that he liked that I liked and we shared several similarities.

"Do you have any siblings?" I asked.

He said, "No, I am an only child. My dad had an outside child, but I am the only one to my parents."

I said, "That is too funny. I am also any only child."

He replied, "I bet you're spoiled and like to get your way."

I retorted, "No, I am not that way, but I am sure that you are. You know those mommas tend to spoil those boys." Of course, he disagreed and we laughed at the many similarities, likes and dislikes.

After a little over two hours had passed, he thought he'd better get back to work.

"I'm going to come to Atlanta next weekend and visit you," Dexter said.

I said, "Yeah, right. I'll believe it when I see it."

He said, "I'm going to make a believer out of you."

Again, I was not even trying to hear, or believe that this man who had just met me was going to drive three hours to visit me the following weekend.

We went back home, and I thought about Dexter all week long. He called me everyday after I returned to Atlanta. When the phone would ring right before I went to bed, that was my good night call. I was getting used to this and looking forward to it. He started to even give me wake up calls in the morning too.

At 8:00 p.m. sharp the following Friday, there was a knock at the door. My heart started racing and my palms became clammy. I peered through the peep hole and my heart skipped a beat, then it fell to my stomach. It was that chocolate brother that had promised that he was coming to visit this weekend. Dexter's eyes were bright and gleaming with excitement.

I opened the door, and there he stood. His physique was just perfect. I stood there in disbelief because I didn't think that he was going to live up to his word.

"Hello", said Dexter.

"Hello," I shyly replied. "Come in," I said almost stuttering.

We embraced each other. His hug was so warm and loving. I felt protected and it actually felt sincere. We looked into each other's eyes and shared a toe curling, passionate kiss. Where had this man come from? Who did he think he was living up to my expectations?

We started to converse about what we would do for the weekend. We were reminded by our growling stomachs that neither of us had eaten dinner. Memorial Drive was live and busy at that time. We had a wide variety of choices. Applebee's won our vote. It was close to where I lived and opened late; therefore, we could eat, talk, and not rush out afterwards.

During dinner, Dexter just stared at me in awe.

I asked him, "What is it?"

He replied, "Oh, nothing, I am just admiring my wonderful company that is beautiful, sweet, and nice." He was still trying to figure things out and so was I. We reminisced about the night we met and how I was just not willing to give him the time of day.

"I thought you were handsome," I admitted, "but I came there for a wedding, not to be matched up with anyone."

He said, "I told Arlene that same night that that's going to be my wife."

I looked at him as if he were a little crazy and said, "Why would you tell her a thing like that? You hadn't even met me yet."

"This is true," he continued. "I hadn't met you and you weren't there to find a man or anything. The Bible says that a man that findeth a wife findeth a good thing. I found my wife. She came to me although she wasn't looking for me."

"Here you go. Look, don't be trying to feed me any lines," I replied.

He said, "I'm not trying to feed you any lines, I just know what I know."

We stayed there after dinner and talked for a long time before we discovered that we were almost the last ones left in the restaurant. When we talked, time just raced by, but at the same time, it appeared to stand still. I felt like there could be some truth to what he was saying, but of course, I was not going to let him tear down the Berlin wall façade that I had built up after we had only known each other for a week. This was our first official date and, I must say, it was a most enjoyable one. We talked for hours on end.

Three years had passed and we continued our long distance calls on the telephone (wake up calls and good night calls). Bellsouth had made a small fortune off of us with our phone bills ranging from $200.00 to $300.00+ on a monthly basis. This was before cell phones became popular with free long distance plans.

In 1998, Dexter asked me to marry him. When I got home from work one day, he had prepared a wonderful candlelight dinner. After dinner we were in the den near the fireplace watching television. He got down on his knee, and formally, and earnestly asked, "Will you marry me?"

I said, "Yes," with tear filled eyes and a knot in my throat.

He moved to Georgia and we bought our first home. It was 1600 square feet with a fenced backyard. We paid off bills that we made prior to each other because we didn't want to owe anyone after we walked down that aisle in thirteen months.

On August 14, 1999, we had the wedding that I dreamed of. The church was brightly decorated with fuchsia and iris (deep purple with hints of blue). The day had arrived. The words that he spoke rang in my ears, "You are going to be my wife. A man that findeth a wife findeth a good thing."

I could not believe that it was coming to pass. I had planned this wedding from start to finish. The wedding party consisted of twelve bridesmaids and twelve groomsmen, two matrons of honor, two best men, three junior bridesmaids, three junior groomsmen, a bell ringer, a Bible carrier, a ring bearer, two flower girls, and of course, the bride and groom. It was held at

41

New Birth Church in Decatur, Georgia. My pastor, Kerwin B. Lee, performed the wedding ceremony. Here we were able to get our 300 guests to enjoy the ceremony then adjourn upstairs to the reception room.

I entered the church with my hairdresser, Keke, singing the solo, "Just For Me" by Karen Clark-Sheard. I must say, I looked and felt like a princess that day. The dress was complete with beading perfectly spaced throughout with a detachable train. My headpiece was fixed as a tiara. As I entered the church, I saw my prince, my knight in shining armor. He looked more handsome than ever in his black tuxedo and vest. As I looked at him, all I could do was smile from ear to ear as I often did in his presence. He starred in awe as he often would do when we were together. God has placed me with my helpmate and this was truly our day that we would never forget.

The reception was awesome too. The wide variety of food and music was a dream come true. We had chicken (fried and baked), macaroni and cheese, green beans, rice pilaf, corn, rolls, tea, punch, and peach cobbler. Everyone enjoyed the food and festivities.

We often reminisce about how we met each other, conversations, and dating like we did when we met. We celebrated our seventh anniversary this year. Seven is the number of completion in the Bible, and we are just waiting and watching God for what He is about to do for us. We have had our ups and downs like any other married couple, but we love each other and are still *in love* with each other.

About the Author

Aleigha A. Butler lives in Atlanta, Georgia. She was born and raised in Gaffney, South Carolina. She attended college and has been residing in Georgia since 1992. While attending DeVry University, she participated in a work study program for the DeKalb County Library System. As a desk clerk, she was introduced to the art of writing and developed a desire to become an author.

Her books and music are produced under the business name of Aleigha's Little Learners. *A Learning Book Just for Me* is the first of many projects that **Aleigha's Little Learners** will bring to the world. The book is available in hard and soft cover editions. Education kits are also available. The education kits include the book, a folder with two worksheets, a pencil, stickers, and a pack of crayons. She plans to have a workbook (that confirms what the children learned in *A Learning Book Just For Me*) ready by early fall. Look for more great products from Aleigha's Little Learners.

E-mail: Aleighaslittlelearners@yahoo.com

Website: www.aleighaslittlelearners.com

8.

LIFE JUST HAPPENS

Anne Haw Holt-Webb

Mom was waiting for me at Broad Street Station. I flew from Tallahassee to Washington, D.C. that week to attend a History Conference, and my guilt convinced me I couldn't come almost a thousand miles and not go a hundred more to pay her a duty visit.

I'd been home almost twenty-four hours and just like clockwork, mom and I had started sniping at each other. I had started to sweat a little, picking up fallen limbs in the yard—working my way down the "to do" list she keeps ready for when one of us comes home for a visit.

Mom came to the door and screeched, "Joyce Anne, you've got a phone call."

I was stumped. I couldn't imagine who could be calling me—in fact, as far as I knew, nobody even knew I was there except for my family. Fuming to myself, I yanked off my gloves and ran in the house to grab the phone—certain something awful had happened.

The voice on the other end said, "It's Bob Webb."

I couldn't think for a minute. I didn't recognize his voice at first—it had been forty—no forty-five years.

I think I said, "Hello."

Then I caught myself and said, "Hello Bob—how wonderful to hear from you. How are you?"

"I'm fine, just fine. It's great to hear your voice."

"Where are you?"

"I'm at home—right here in Green Springs. I came home for my high school reunion and your big sister was there. She told me you were at home."

I said something—I don't remember what—he interrupted.

"I'd like to take you to lunch tomorrow."

"That would be nice. I—I'd love to see you."

"Can I pick you up at your mother's at eleven thirty?"

I'm not sure what I said, but I know I agreed. I dropped the phone back on its cradle and stood there staring at it. My hands were trembling. I remember the first time I saw him.

The old Chevy roared to a stop not ten feet away from me. It had shiny black paint and gangster whitewalls splashed with globs of red Louisa County mud from the awful road to our farm. I sat up and pulled the quilt I'd been sunbathing on up around my shoulders and crossed my arms to hide my overgrown boobs.

The car was full—I could see my sister's frizzy black hair in the back seat. I heard her talking about her triple date with a new boyfriend for the whole week. His name was Bob something or other.

The guy in the front seat opened the door closest to me and sort of unwound himself from the car. He reached around to help my sister out of the back seat. I saw the gleam in my sister's eye when she noticed me sitting there trying to hide my barely covered figure under a quilt out in the hot sunshine. As soon as she got her feet on the ground she caught the guy's arm and turned toward me.

"Well, blast." I muttered to myself. She knew how embarrassed I got—but she couldn't let such a chance pass.

I couldn't do a thing but sit still. I screwed up my courage and pasted a smile on my face. When I looked up I thought, "He has the kindest blue eyes…"

I forgot to be embarrassed and held out my hand. Our fingers barely touched. My sister was jabbering away about something, but I couldn't make out a word she was saying.

I can still remember how he smiled at me and said, "Well, hello there." It plain took my breath away.

My sister stopped talking for a minute or two. I remember blessing the silence for a minute, and then she sounded almost as if she was growling, "If you two don't mind—I'm ready to go in the house. Come on Bobby, I want to introduce you to mama and daddy."

When he turned away to look down at her, it felt sort of like I would fall over, right there on top of that doggone sunbathing quilt.

My sister almost lost it when she saw me and Bobby walking around together at school. She knew it meant we were going steady. She glared at me all the way home on the school bus.

I ran ahead home to give her time to cool off on the way, but she caught up and reached out to grab me by the hair about the time we walked into our yard. I was fourteen and she was sixteen, but she never had a chance. I held her down with my knees in her back and tried to pull out hands full of her curly black hair until her screams brought mama running out of the house with a broom.

Bob and I were sweethearts until we were seventeen. Oh my—were we sweethearts, but that was a long time ago.

He arrived at Mom's house a little early, but that was all right. I'd been dressed and ready for at least an hour. When I opened the door and looked into those blue eyes I stood there smiling, not saying a word.

He said, "Well, hello there."

I couldn't for the life of me figure out how we managed to get apart all those years ago. I guess life just happens. I remember I went to work in Richmond, and he went into the Air Force. Both of us had great careers, married, and had children and grandchildren. But it felt as if we hadn't been apart a day. We've hardly been apart an hour since.

<u>About the Author</u>

Anne Haw Holt-Webb is from Richmond, Virginia. She graduated from Piedmont Virginia Community College in Charlottesville in 1987 and Mary Baldwin College in Staunton, Virginia, in 1989. She lived and worked in the Charlottesville/Central Virginia area for almost thirty years.

Anne now lives in Tallahassee, Florida, where she attained her Ph.D. in History at Florida State University in 2005. Her dissertation is on the early history of Florida Prisons.

Her recent publications include the following:
Riding Fence, novel, ISBN 0803498012, Avalon Books, NY, 2006
Blanco Sol, novel, ISBN 0803496001, Avalon Books, NY, 2005
Kendrick, novel, ISBN 0803406508, Avalon Books, NY, 2004
Silver Creek, novel, ISBN 0803496001 Avalon Books, 2003
My Friend: In a Grain of Truth, Apollo's Lyre, New Ink, Vol. I, Issue 3, March 10, 2003.
Parenting From Inside, Handbook and Curriculum, Florida Department of Corrections, Programs Department.
Reading Family Ties for Men, Video script produced by Florida Department of Corrections.

E-mail: aholt@garnet.acns.fsu.edu

9.

LOVE BEGETS LOVE

Patricia Woodside

Taller than anyone I'd ever met, his long legs easily supported his six-foot-seven frame. The strain of his pale gray tuxedo when he adjusted his stance, his arms held downward, hands clasped at his center and legs slightly apart, hinted at the muscular, athletic physique hidden beneath the fabric. I nervously two-stepped toward him, concentrating less on the music filling the church and more on not falling and embarrassing myself. He stood tall at the altar awaiting my arrival, a dark chocolate Adonis.

Butterflies flitted about my insides. I ran through my invisible checklist one last time. Maid of honor for one of my oldest and dearest friends, my "partner in crime," the woman who'd introduced me to the Wendy's Frosty, I'd morphed from my normally reserved self into a mini drill sergeant to insure that she had her perfect day. That included the minor tiff I'd had with the wedding coordinator just before marching down the aisle, who seemed to think the flower girls' white lace gloves, inadvertently left behind in the church basement, weren't that important. Everything was important. Everything from the gloves to the rose petals on the white plastic runner to the birdseed that we'd pelt the happy couple with afterwards. If Fran wanted it, she was going to have it. The devil is in the details. I knew one day she'd do the same for me.

Nothing left to do but make it just a few more steps. *God, please don't let me trip on this carpet*, I prayed as I neared the end of my solo procession. I'd always loved the richness of the thick, ruby-red church carpet except, that is, when I had to walk on it with all eyes on me. Reaching my designated spot, I smiled at him across the altar. His serious demeanor remained unchanged.

A short time later, I gently placed my hand in the crook of his elbow and together we recessed down the aisle and out the church. I used his strength to eliminate any worries about tripping or falling. Outside, we stood together, greeting family and friends until finally we were introduced. His large hand swallowed mine.

"Nice to meet you. How're you doing?" I asked.

"Nice to meet you," he responded.

Not real meaningful conversation. Pretty tepid actually. We exchanged pleasantries, him asking about my life in Cincinnati, me asking about his life in Baton Rouge, and his Division I basketball career.

Bernard, the best man and groom's brother, towered over my petite, five-foot-two frame. We'd both flown in for the occasion, but I'd arrived too late for most of the previous night's wedding rehearsal and there hadn't been time to meet before the ceremony.

A few years away from home had boosted my confidence. I came from a small family in a small, blue-collar town. Now college-educated and a working professional, I considered myself mature and worldly, not easily impressed. Yet, Bernard's reserved manner belied a fire that got my attention.

Too bad he's a couple of years younger than me, I mused. Besides, didn't becoming Fran's brother-in-law make him off limits?

Fran and I were so close that now Bernard seemed like family too. Anyway, he wasn't interested. The memory of that day that grafted itself to my mind involved him and his newly married brother tuning the limousine's miniature television set to the Yankees game as we pulled away from the church.

"Pat, you won't believe this!"

Stretched on the sofa, the phone to my ear, I wondered what good news Fran had to share. Several years married, she'd been blessed with twin boys a few short months ago.

"I'm pregnant. Again."

"What?" I dropped the TV remote and barely managed to stay on the couch.

"Are you sure? When are you due?"

"Yes, we're sure. Sometime around the twins' first birthday. Can you believe it?"

Stunned, I congratulated my friend. I knew I didn't fully comprehend the magnitude of expecting one's third child when the first two little ones—beautiful, rambunctious boys—had not yet turned one. In the midst of her happiness, a familiar pang tugged at my heart. I too wished to be a wife and mother, in addition to pursing my career, but I knew that if it happened for me, it would be in God's timing and in His way. I'd had enough misfires of my own that I'd recently decided to leave my love life in God's hands.

A year later, I flew home at Thanksgiving for my goddaughter's christening. After attending the church where Fran and I grew up, I joined her and her husband at their current church for the ceremony that would conclude the morning service.

God, faith, and church defined our lives. Church birthed our personal relationships, our sense of community, our education, and our entertainment. Fran's father pastored our "home" church and her father-in-law pastored her current church. Even if there hadn't been a christening, whenever I went home for a visit, I tried to make a point of attending both services.

A spirited worship service heightened by lively music and rousing singing welcomed me. I quickly seated myself near the rear, so as not to disturb the saints in the throes of praise. Upon settling myself on the pew, I surveyed the front of the church. My eyes rested on the gentleman playing drums. Fine. *Who was that brother?* I didn't recall him from previous visits. I made a mental note to ask Fran after the service.

"Oooh, come here, and let me look at you! You look too good for words!"

"How's everything in...where are you now? In Ohio?"

"Baby, give me a hug! I hear good things about you!"

These and other words of welcome and encouragement flowed easily from those who shook my hand, hugged me, and twirled me around after the service. As much as I loved and took pride in owning my own house, progressing in my career, and feeling established in the Midwest, it always felt good to be back home. And, on this particular occasion, the care I'd taken with my appearance warranted the praise.

In recent months, I'd committed to get in shape. I'd worked hard to drop thirty pounds. I blushed with pride when complimented on my toned and trim form. The skirt of my ivory Ann Taylor crepe suit fell slightly above my knees, showing off my shapely calves, accompanied by a matching military-style jacket that fell (almost) flat across my abdomen adorned with large gold buttons down the front, on the epaulets, and at the wrists. Gold earrings and choker, off-white hose, and golden tan Etienne Aigner pumps completed my outfit. I hated covering up my attire but the frosty November winds swirling about dictated good sense. I tightened my velvet-trimmed overcoat around me.

When I finished buttoning my coat, the handsome drummer stood before me. He introduced himself. I nearly fell over. Bernard Woodside! The younger brother of Fran's husband, Tyrone, and their best man, had turned into a sophisticated, self-assured man. Maybe age truly was nothin' but a number!

Buoyed that Bernard had noticed me, I tried not to make too much of it, although I liked the attention. I'd recently started dating someone I'd met at the Black MBA annual conference. Marc was a nice guy. We shared common goals and a common faith. Was he the answer to my prayers? I didn't know but I preferred being a one-man woman. Bernard and I spoke politely for a few minutes and went our separate ways.

Later that day, I hung out at Fran's home, eager to spend time with her family. Standing in her blue and white country kitchen, she whispered conspiratorially to me.

"Guess who asked about you?"

"Who?" No possibilities came to my mind.

"Bernard." A familiar glee entered Fran's eyes. I could see her dusting off her matchmaking gloves. We were both big romantics and if there were a possibility of a love connection, Fran would go above and beyond the call of duty to make a match.

"He asked for your phone number, but I told him I had to check with you first."

I smiled what I hoped was a disinterested smile, even though I knew Fran could see right through me.

"You can give it to him. I'll be surprised if he calls."

"He'll call."

He didn't call. A month later, I returned to New York to spend the Christmas week with my mother before heading to Minneapolis to spend New Year's with my friend from the conference. Again, I attended Pastor Woodside's church.

The briskness of the air blew through my bones, propelling me into the church. I expected to see Bernard, but since he hadn't called, I figured he had no real interest. As I slid into the wooden pew, our eyes met, he was again vigorously playing the drums. He never missed a beat although I felt my heart skip one. Time to get "the 411" as to what was going on in his life, to place in my mental filing cabinet. For future reference. Just in case.

As before, after service, I went to Fran's house. After we'd eaten and played with the children, who should show up but Bernard? He wore his navy full-length wool coat pulled up around his ears, nursing a slight cold, but he looked as good as I'd remembered. The man had style.

"What are you doing for Christmas?" The stuffiness in his head slurred his words a little bit.

"Spending time with my mother, opening gifts, the usual."

"Do you want to go to the movies?" *A date?* My pulse sped up.
I assumed the two of us would finally have a chance to get to know one another away from the watchful eyes of church folks.

Not quite. Bernard arrived to pick me up for the movie in a gray Cadillac. He held the door open so that I could seat myself.

"Hey Pat!" I glanced into the back seat, surprised to see additional passengers.

"Hey, Tabreeca. Charmise. Merry Christmas!" I fondly acknowledged two of Bernard's sisters.

"This is Craig, Toni's husband." Tabreeca gestured to the gentleman who sat beside them. He wore an impish grin, clearly amused by the unfolding scene. Charmise looked miffed.

"He said he had to pick someone up, but we didn't know it was you." Tabreeca rattled on, her infectious manner ever present.

"Yes, that would be nice."

"You're going to the movies too?" I struggled to clarify the situation.

"Bernard always takes me out for my birthday," Charmise, the Christmas baby, answered.

His two younger sisters and a brother-in-law? Strange but hey, at minimum, it was a chance to enjoy a free movie. Maybe I had misinterpreted Bernard's signals. Oh well. Shaking off my disappointment, I focused on having a good time. We did. We sat away from our chaperones and even held hands. We had a nice time, and I agreed to meet him for lunch the next day.

The waitress scribbled on her pad as she placed our menus under her arm and moved across the aisle to another customer. The lunchtime rush in full swing, the din of the increasing crowd made it difficult to hear. Sitting back against the worn leather of the Friendly's booth, Bernard dipped his chin.

"I'm not looking for a casual date or a new girlfriend."

My breath caught. I knew what he meant without him saying the words. He wanted to find his wife.

This was serious, as we both came from a background that emphasized "until death do us part." Talk about an icebreaker! This was only our second date and our first real conversation. We'd only begun to get to know one another. I knew that he'd been engaged before but didn't know what had happened. Yet, I felt oddly drawn to him. The soothing yet authoritative tenor of his voice gripped me. He had dark brown eyes that seemed to absorb my every word like a thirsty sponge.

"I understand." I looked him squarely in his eyes. We were on the same page even if we used few words to express our shared sentiment. We continued our lunch, laughing and talking, sharing tidbits about ourselves over cups of steaming clam chowder. Would "enjoyable but unusual" describe all of our dates?

I had four days before my scheduled departure. We spent time together each day. I grew increasingly uncomfortable with the idea of flying to spend time with someone else. I'd begun to have real feelings for Bernard. I wanted to stay and get to know him better, but I also felt obligated to keep my commitment, not to mention that my airline tickets were already paid for, and I was strapped for cash. For his part, Bernard made it clear that he didn't want me to leave, but that it was my decision. I figured we'd keep in touch. Everything would sort itself out in due time.

From the moment, the plane landed in snowy Minneapolis, I knew I'd made a big mistake. I felt uneasy. I had this horrible sense that I'd screwed up big time. Marc met me at the airport. The feeling that I was spiraling into a dark abyss only grew in intensity as we made our way to his condo, met his friends at a seafood restaurant for dinner, and then returned to his place.

"What's wrong? Something is bothering you," Marc queried gently, certain that somehow things had gone off kilter.

"I can't explain it." I was still sorting it all out in my head because I'd never before had such a strong sense of being in the wrong place at the wrong time. How could I tell him without hurting his feelings and looking completely foolish?

"Please try. You barely spoke at dinner, although my friends tried to include you. This is not like you."

They had tried, but I'd been distracted, not interested in the playful banter and philosophical discussions that accompanied the meal. I sat silently. Unease evolved into nausea. My skin tingled to a degree I'd never experienced. When it became obvious I wouldn't or couldn't say more, he rose and led the way into his guest room. He showed me where everything was and told me what time he'd be leaving for work the next day. Then he said good night, leaving me to my misery.

After a fitful night and a breakfast accompanied by stony silence, I watched as Marc stormed out to go to work. I'd disappointed him and embarrassed him before his friends. I felt badly. I knew he'd be even unhappier with my next move, but I knew it was the right one. As soon as the lock clicked behind him, I raced to the phone.

"Fran?"

"Pat, what's wrong? What's going on?" We'd always been able to read each other even when we were miles apart.

"I'm coming back, but I need your help."

"Tell me what you need me to do."

"I'm going to check the flights. As soon as I can get something, I'll call you." Snow fell in thick clumps on top of the

54

already covered ground. Even if I could somehow afford the flight change, the weather remained a potential wrench in my plan.

"Can you or someone pick me up from the airport?"

"Don't worry about that. Someone will be there."

I booked the first available flight out and re-routed the third leg of my trip to go from LaGuardia to Cincinnati, to the tune of nearly one thousand dollars, maxing out my last remaining credit card. I didn't care. There was something between Bernard and I, something special. Even my mother, who generally had no opinion about my relationships, had commented on it. I knew I had to see this through. Was I the wife he sought? Was he the husband I'd asked God for? I didn't know, but I knew that we had to explore the possibility.

When I called Marc to tell him of my plans, he sniffed, asked me to leave the key under the mat, and hung up. I didn't blame him, and I did feel badly but that was that. Not wanting to waste another moment on our soured relationship, I hastily packed and made my way to the airport.

I made my way through the New York concourse and down to the luggage area. I retrieved my bags and waited with bated breath. I expected Fran; I hoped for Bernard. Sure enough, my eyes fell upon a tall drink of cool water coming toward me. Bernard strode confidently, almost swaggering. Asking only whether I'd gotten all of my things, to which I nodded, he took my overstuffed garment bag, turned, and led the way out of the airport.

We rode in silence. I wasn't sure what to think. He'd come for me, but I assumed the man had an ego, and I'd bruised it. Bernard wasn't saying much. Clearly he wasn't going to make this easy. I apologized for leaving, but he cut off my explanation.

"Doesn't matter."

We stopped at a nearby diner to grab a bite. Slowly but surely, over French fries and hamburgers, the icy silence thawed. By the time we headed home, we were laughing again and made plans to go out the next day. Bernard and I picked up where we left off, spending time together every day, right up to New Years' Eve.

New Year's Eve loomed clear but frigid. I'd spent the day racing around Green Acres Mall to find a memorable outfit. I'd packed clothes that were more than sufficient, but I wanted enchanting. I wanted to implant deep, lasting impressions before I left. That night, I wore a black velvet skirt suit studded with bronze sequins, black stockings, and black sling back heels. He wore a black suit that covered him as though he were born in it.

Together we attended Watch Night Service at his father's church, to thank God for the closing year and to utter prayers for the new one. Following the service, we went back to my mother's home and talked, neither of us wanting the night to end. Once again, I'd be flying away from him the next day.

Bernard drove me to the airport. Inside, he purchased a dozen roses and a teddy bear from a vendor at the gate entrance. I hadn't been this reluctant to return to Ohio, where I'd made a home for myself, where the majority of my friends lived and where I was a semester short of completing my master's degree, since my father had died five years earlier. At that moment, I wanted nothing more than to stay. With Bernard.

Following my departure, marathon phone conversations filled our nights. We poured out our hearts to each other over the long distance lines, oblivious to the per minute charges. I found it difficult to concentrate at work or school. Bernard invaded and commandeered my thoughts. So little time had passed since Christmas but it seemed like a lifetime. On January 9th, just seven days after we'd parted, sixteen days after our first date, I heard those life-altering words:

"Will you marry me?"

Without hesitation, I answered, "Yes."

Exactly six years to the day, from when Bernard and I met, as best man and maid of honor for his brother and my best friend, we again stood at an altar surrounded by family and friends. This time, Fran and Tyrone stood beside us as we exchanged our vows, delighted to pledge our lives to one another as husband and wife.

Fifteen years and four children later, Bernard and I have endured our share of ups and downs, of mountaintops, bumpy roads and life's little surprises, but we remain committed in love. Sometimes weddings lead to other weddings. Love begets love.

About the Author

Patricia Woodside has been immersed in a lifelong love affair with books. After pursuing a career and establishing her family, Patricia decided to explore writing. She uncapped her pen with family life articles for online newsletters and book reviews for online publications, including SORMAG magazine and Fresh Fiction. Early contest success included selection for the as-yet-unreleased inspirational anthology, *Hope Lives On*, by Obadiah Press, in which Patricia shares how her faith enabled her to cope with the stillbirth of her daughter, Stephanie. Recently, Patricia was published in the nationally distributed *True Romance* magazine. She also has sold a short holiday romance to e-publisher, The Wild Rose Press. And Patricia is working on her first full-length novel.

A native New Yorker, Patricia and her family left behind wintry snowdrifts for the balmy breezes of Tampa, Florida. She continues to apply her information technology expertise for a local retail conglomerate. With her husband, Bernard, she leads Global Harvest International Ministries. They have three sons: Bernard Benjamin, Trevor, and Phillip.

Blog: http://readinnwritin.blogspot.com

E-mail: pwriter1@yahoo.com

10.

MY FIRST LOVE

Vien Jernigan

"Okay, just get your keys out and if they try anything funny, just gouge their eyes out! I mean, they look nice and everything but you never know," my friend, April, scolded me.

Romantic or not, believe it or not, this is how I met Justin, my college sweetheart of fourteen years. It was all a great big surprise really. The year was 1992, my first week at the University of Florida. I was scared and excited. Coming from a very sheltered background, for the first time I finally had some independence. I cried only for the first couple of hours that I was alone, missing all the noise of my family around me.

My mother made two crucial comments, "Please don't get killed, and don't be in a rush to find your husband."

I said, "Mother, please. I am not interested. I am going to be a businesswoman for crying out loud. Besides, I have some partying to do first."

With that being said, my poor mother almost fainted from fear of what might happen when I am left on my own. Concerning the former comment about getting killed, there had been a spree of murders in Gainesville and everyone at UF, at that time, was on high alert. Fortunately, I was not in danger of that kind, but my heart was in imminent danger of falling desperately in love. I hate it when my mom is right.

That first weekend, I went to a luau thrown by a college Christian group called Intervarsity. I was looking cute in a floral tank and white shorts, my hair loosely pulled back. I was having a great time meeting people and stuffing my face when I saw three guys heading over towards my friend and me. They were really nice and, to be honest, I was more interested in one of my future husband's tall friends than him.

We all talked through the evening, and I noticed Justin continually looking at me. He looked strange to me at first, but he won me over with how sincere and considerate he was. He said he was majoring in Russian and was president of the Russian club. Justin was a junior, so he was two years ahead of me. We had a great time at the party and the guys offered to give my friend and me a lift back to our dorm. And that's when April almost flipped her lid. Luckily, they dropped us off at our dorm like complete gentlemen. Justin gave me his phone number but because I was not interested in the Russian club, I turned around and handed it to April. Upon reflection, I felt terrible about that, but Justin would later say that the fact that I even took his number was a sign to him that he actually had a great chance.

Justin called me the next day. We talked easily and he was just so sweet. He wanted to know everything about me and was interested in everything I had to say. He cared about my life and me. I mentioned that I didn't have any Amy Grant music and he surprised me later that same night when he stopped by and had made a tape for me. It really made an impression on me that he thought so much about me and went out of his way. The list goes on for miles of all the ways that Justin has blown me away with how much effort and love he has spoken of, but also shown me in actions.

On my first day of college, as soon as I got home from class, Justin called to see how I liked it. I can't tell you how awesome it felt to have someone care and pay attention to me while I was away from my family for the first time. Pretty soon, Justin became my home away from home. He became my family. He showed up early in the morning at the bottom of my stairs with a big bright welcoming smile, had breakfast with me and then walked me to my class. Anything that he had to do became secondary—his classes or errands. He was mainly focused and concerned with me first.

Coming from a big adopted family where I had to learn to share everything—especially attention—and where I have learned that to be the authority figure was not the priority, I am propelled into a new world of being made to feel special and prized. It was unfamiliar, yet so welcomed. Being with Justin, I felt completely accepted, loved, sexy, and happy. I was happier than I had ever felt before. All of this was new to me.

I only found out later, from his friends, that Justin ran and chased down the bus in the mornings so he could make it to campus to see me before I headed off to class. His apartment buddies were sometimes furious with him because he borrowed their cars and was gone all day wooing me. I was not popular at the apartment and they even took the picture of me that I had given to Justin and drew a mustache on it. Justin was furious about that, which rarely happens.

His friends are great and we eventually would get along just fine, but it was a bumpy start. They felt I had taken him away from them and that he was being inconsiderate of their feelings. Really I think maybe they were just jealous that he had a serious girlfriend before any of them. They complained about us making them feel uncomfortable by being attached at the hip and by our PDA (public displays of affection), but in the long run, they realized how we loved each other and that we cared about them too. This led them to support us after all.

Attention is great, but when it borders on stalker territory it is no longer so fun. Justin soon got a job filing student records at the stadium. He managed to find my social security number and my class schedule. So, on a campus of 40,000 people, everywhere I went, there was Justin's smiling face beaming at me. It was cute at first, but then it got annoying and even scary. What was even scarier was that he was really starting to grow on me. Never let anyone tell you stalking is not a viable option to hooking up. Yeah, that's right; I was falling in love with my stalker. That's all I can say. You can't always explain or control matters of the heart. Things happen as they may and that's that.

Honestly, I wasn't attracted to him at first, but as I got to know him even better, he became increasingly and incredibly sexy and irresistible. I liked the way his mind worked, how he was able to see things in a pure way and communicate that. Sexiest of all his parts was his heart. I had never met someone so humble and kind hearted. He always sees good in people. It's the thing I love most about him.

No matter how big or how long my classes were, when I came out there was Justin, waiting to escort me anywhere I needed to go. One day, it was raining and I thought for sure he wouldn't be there, but sure enough, there he was hovering under a tree in the rain waiting for me to come out.

We disagree on when our first date was exactly. Justin said it was when we went to see *Sister Act* pretty soon after we first met, but I told him I only considered him a friend then, and that's why I was telling him about all these cute guys I saw on campus. Then he said that maybe our first date was when we went to eat at the Szechuan Panda restaurant, and I said, "Nope, I wouldn't wear shorts on a first date."

I remember our first date being much later, when we went to see *The Last of the Mohicans*. I know this is true because that is when I started feeling more than just friendship for him, and I freaked because he tried to put his hand on my back on the way out of the theatre, and I bolted. It was very "poor college student cute" when he drove us through the drive thru at McDonald's for fries and cokes afterwards.

I remember the first time we held hands. We were waiting for Justin's ride to pick him up in front of my dorm. It was late autumn, and it was getting nippy. I had a sweater on, but Justin was shivering. I offered to rub his hands to help keep them warm, but he kept hanging onto my arm and rubbing it. Soon a friend of ours walked up, and I yanked my arm away from him like he had a disease. I was so embarrassed. We went to a play called *The Rainmaker* a couple weeks later, and by that time I was so smitten with him I didn't care who saw us caressing each other's arms (among other things) during the play.

Justin, my stalker-turned-best friend, continued coming by for three months. He started coming to my Bible study as well as leading one of his own (for which he tried to recruit me and was extremely persistent in his follow-up efforts). Our Bible study group had Thanksgiving dinner together and it became obvious to everyone that we had something going on when we happily shared one piece of pumpkin pie. Since our fellowship was considered a mating ground, no one was surprised. We had a great time with our friends playing Jenga, singing worship songs, and studying the Bible. My bond with Justin was intensified because it included and was enhanced by the presence and anointing of Jesus' love and purity. That night when Justin walked me home, we sat down on a bench and talked and laughed and he asked if he could kiss me.

I said, "Yes, but only on the cheek."

Man, oh man, was he persistent!!! He kept wearing me down until I gave in. Me, of prudish Asian descent, and even stricter Southern Baptist morals. Our first kiss was really and truly both of our first kisses. We kissed in the dark, on a bench in front of my dorm, and then I felt wetness on my head and my arm. I thought for sure he couldn't have that much salvia. With my eyes closed and all these feelings coursing through me, I wasn't sure. Soon, I realized the sprinklers had switched on, and we were both drenched. Our first kiss ended with the sprinkler chasing us off.

Our first kiss was sweet and liberating and so romantic. I enjoyed it immensely while it was going on but afterwards when I got back to my dorm, I felt dirty. I don't know if it was just fear or that I took pride in my purity, but I felt like I had given away too much, and that I had been violated. I tried to clean myself. I scrubbed my face and brushed my teeth thoroughly three or four times. I really wanted to puke. I felt so conflicted that night trying to go to sleep—wanting the excitement and intimacy but hating the change in me. I wanted to be both a woman and a girl. I wanted to know the newness of everything, but I was not yet ready to let go of the girl in me that I was so comfortable with and fond of. *Am I really ready for this? Love—is it all that they say that it is? Will I regret it forever if I let it flow in freely or in earnest fear, push its tidal waves back?*

God has blessed us with such an amazing relationship because neither of us had dated anyone seriously before. We were each other's first relationship, first boyfriend/girlfriend, first kiss, first love, first everything. We were so exclusive and it felt fabulous. I highly recommend waiting for your one true love and quite possibly your one and only soul mate. We dated for five years before marrying and consummating our love on our honeymoon night. A feat only possible by the grace of God. We are both Jesus freaks and loving God comes before loving each other or pleasure or sex. It wasn't for a lack of trying, though.

Some nights before we said goodbye and he was leaving to go to his dorm instead of staying with me, we had felt ready to toss faith and everything else out the window and just get on down to the nasty. But many times, Jesus has literally saved us from ourselves and stood between us, helping us to wait until the time is right and good and honorable.

The fact that Justin loved culture and language made it advantageous that we are from different backgrounds. It honored me so that he checked out books and tapes on Vietnam, the country, the people. He taught me things about my own heritage. We both took a Vietnamese class together and Justin can speak, write, and read it better than me. It's a pathetic story, and I shouldn't retell it too often. That is how Justin has won my parents over too. They were fuming that first and foremost their little girl was seeing a boy instead of focusing 110% on studying, but on top of that offense, she is seeing a non-Asian. Oh, for the love of God!

They inevitably found out about Justin. I came home for the Christmas holiday wearing a gold and diamond bracelet and because I was such a goody two shoes, I was able to get away with a simple "My friend gave it to me." There was no avoiding it, however, when they dropped in to visit me at the university on Valentine's Day and there was a huge bouquet of red long-stemmed roses on my desk. When my parents first met Justin, it was deafeningly silent and awkward. The only acknowledgement my father made was, "What's your name?" and the equally amicable, "How old are you?"

Being Buddhist, my dad was superstitious and wanted to make sure that Justin's and my signs and ages were compatible. The collision of East meets West is interesting, but Justin was able to win them over by being extremely optimistic and kind (and learning to speak the language helped tremendously). They couldn't badmouth him any more.

It was most interesting when I went to visit Justin's family in a small town. Quite honestly, I feared for my life around some of the backward people there. Luckily, not all perceptions were correct and I ended up pleasantly surprised at how friendly and hospitable the people there really were.

Justin and I share many things in common. We love the same music basically: the oldies, the 80s, but I lean towards dance while he enjoys James Taylor. We both love to eat and travel and experience different cultures and enjoy a lot of time alone with just the two of us. We also have lots of differences that we fight about such as leadership and preparation, but we have a willingness to listen and care enough to try to meet each other's needs.

Justin says he fell in love at first sight and knew he wanted to marry me, but for me, it took a lot of convincing. I had tried breaking up with him countless times. One night, we had the big talk. I told him he was suffocating me and that I needed some space. I wanted to see other people, and I didn't want to be tied down. He agreed. So he stayed away and didn't call for a whopping total of one day. He then had the nerve to call me the next day and ask whether or not that was enough space. I tell you, the man wore me down until I gave in!

My college sweetheart and I have seen many triumphs: getting our own apartment, starting careers, pets, kids, vacations, and struggles, such as finances, temptation, sickness, social, and even emotional problems. We are focused, devoted, and loyal. He has always believed in and supported me no matter who, no matter what the issue, and no matter how the chips may fall.

We have been together for fourteen years now. Our family has been enriched by our friends here and abroad. Before I met Justin, I was like a flower bud, eager to grow and bloom. With his love, attention, and commitment, I am able to receive the support to nourish and grow. He provides the grounding soil, the water, and sun so I can finally bloom radiantly. The bench where we had our first kiss still reminds me of the changing and enduring power of love. At first, it had no special significance but because it has been christened as the site of our first physical expression of love, it holds profound importance. Over the years it started just as an old wooden bench, but it has been renovated and now it is newer, bigger and better with stronger legs made of concrete.

<u>About the Author</u>

Vien Jernigan was born in Vietnam during the war in the 1970's. She is now a stay-at-home mother of two preschool boys. She has been married to her husband for nine years, although she count it as fourteen, since 1992, because they have dated each other exclusively since the day they first met. She lives in Tallahassee where her husband is finishing his Ph.D. in education. She writes in her spare time.

Currently, she is working on three books. One is the story of how her family escaped communist Vietnam and came to America. She believes that even if it is not published, it will be worthwhile because it is a part of her children's history and legacy. The second book will be about Vietnamese children's stories. Another will be about her own children's mixed heritage.

Her hobbies are reading, watching movies, walking, dancing, and bargain shopping. One of her favorite fantasies is that someday one of her inventions will be patented. Either that or that she will be able to land a job that she will be happy with—either a nonprofit such as the Peace Corps, as a Red Cross volunteer, or to open her own small business.

E-mail:　　Jernigans3@yahoo.com

11.

NOTHING IN COMMON

Sherille Fisher

I don't know where to begin. It all happened so early in my life. I'll just start with my senior year. During my high school days, I did well until my senior year when I started cutting up. When I say that I don't mean being bad, I mean just not doing my class assignment like I should. I didn't put any effort in my studies. I didn't plan on going to college so all I was trying to do was pass.

Before I knew it, I was failing, and I didn't have time to catch up. So on that hot and humid day in Miami, Florida, in 1982, as I stood outside of Miami Dade Community College waiting to march with 700 other high school seniors, I was very sad. I marched that night, but that's all I did. I didn't get my diploma, because I needed a few more credits.

I enrolled in summer school and actually graduated in January 1983. Well, while I was in summer school, my cousin, Gilda, asked me if I wanted to visit her in Houston, Texas. At first I said, "I'll think about it." I was working at Burger King, but I wanted to get a job at a clothing store when I graduated. I did get an interview at some clothing shop in the mall, but I didn't get hired.

When it got close to graduation, I called my cousin and told her that I wanted to visit. I only planned to get a job and stay two or three months even though she said I could stay longer. Gilda heard that I didn't want to go to college, and she planned to change my mind.

Before I left for Texas, I ran into this real nice guy at the mall that I knew from my childhood. We exchanged telephone numbers and started going out on dates. I really liked him. One day he told me that he was in the Army, and guess were he was stationed? You guessed it, Texas. I couldn't believe it! That made me want to go to Texas that much more.

Before he left at the end of December 1982, we became an exclusive couple. I soon left for Texas, in January 1983, the Saturday before Super Bowl Sunday. I remember the game because the Miami Dolphins were playing the Washington Redskins.

I told my family goodbye and planned to return sometime in March. I arrived in Houston, Texas, about 9:00 that night. My cousin and her husband greeted me as I got off the airplane. We hugged and went straight to the grocery store so that I could get the food I liked and from there we went to their apartment.

They lived in the Southwest part of Houston. I remember being awestruck as I saw the beautiful Houston skyline as we got closer to downtown Houston after leaving Intercontinental Airport, now called Bush Intercontinental.

We talked and reminisced about old times. It was easy to adjust to my new setting. Before I went to bed, they asked me if I wanted to go to church with them the next morning. I said yes because I always enjoyed attending church.

The next morning we got up, and I quickly got dressed. We went to a Methodist Church called Parkcrest located in a predominately Black part of Houston, called South Park. My cousin and her husband lived near the Galleria, a diverse part of Houston.

When we got to the church, we went down a long hallway, past a daycare center with a kitchen next to a small chapel located in the back. I noticed a much larger church in the front that my cousin said was being renovated so that they could worship there later in the year. I enjoyed the service and the small congregation was very friendly. I learned later that most of the members were family and close friends.

After church, Gilda and her husband, Thomas, introduced me to a nice young man. I must say I did notice him during worship service. I was glad that I had a chance to talk to him. It turned out that he and Thomas attended the same law school, Thurgood Marshall School of Law, on the campus of Texas Southern University. We shook hands and continued to talk as my cousin and her husband walked ahead of us.

He said, "I would love to show you around Houston."

I gladly accepted his invitation. But, the funniest thing came out of his mouth next. When I think about it even today it cracks me up. He told me, "I like your mustache."

I figured he was looking pretty hard to notice the little fuzz above my lip. Being fair-complexioned, I could not cover my red cheeks. I was just blushing my butt off. We laughed it off, and I said, "I hope to see you soon."

There was something about this young man I really liked. What he said was corny, but I have a sense of humor so that didn't bother me at all. I left with my cousin and her husband to get ready for the super bowl game. Gilda made her homemade pizza and it was delicious. We invited Harrison, the young man from church, to come over, but he declined.

Late that night, my boyfriend called, and we talked about his upcoming trip to Houston. I soon discovered how far away he was in the big state of Texas. He was in El Paso, which is over 600 miles from Houston. That was a lot of distance between us. This would be my first long distance relationship, but I was willing to give it a try. He was such a nice young man, and we were the same age. Most of the guys I dated were my age. I was only eighteen so having boyfriends was kind of new to me. I really didn't take that sort of stuff too seriously.

At that time in my life, I was ninety eight pounds of skin and bones, and was wearing my hair short and curly. All I cared to do was read and talk on the phone, but I didn't get to talk much on the phone because most of my family and friends lived in Miami. I was having reservations about my long distance relationship. That kind of stuff lasts when you're in love; I wasn't.

On Monday, Gilda took me job-hunting, as per my request. She really wanted me to go to college, and we talked about it during the whole time I was seeking employment. She and her husband were both college graduates, and I understood that all she wanted was the best for me.

That very day, I got a job at a Burger King not far from my cousin's apartment. I had previously worked there while I was in high school in Miami, so I applied again. I tried the mall first, but the places I went to were not accepting applications. So Burger King was where I went and they hired me. I worked the night shift, leaving day open for college, should I have a change of heart. I liked the nightshift because it gave me my daytime to read. I also did some writing to my family back in Miami, and I wrote my boyfriend too.

The apartment was near an ice cream parlor, a card shop, and a Chinese restaurant. I would sometimes walk to get whatever I wanted while Gilda and Thomas were gone. I enjoyed having time to myself.

One day, I visited a friend from back home who was in the hospital. He had injured his leg playing football for Texas Southern University. There were about five young men visiting with him when I arrived. I got acquainted with one of the young men from Homestead, Florida. We exchanged telephone numbers and talked on the telephone. He asked me out, and I said 'yes.'

I was off that Friday, and it was Tuesday. He said, "I'll call you Thursday regarding the time of our date."

I waited as Thursday came, then Friday, and no telephone call, I didn't care. My cousin and her husband had a date with another couple that lived next to the Texas Southern University campus. Well, I could have easily stayed at their place and read a good book, but I wanted to go out too. Something told me to give Harrison a call. He was the handsome young man I met at church. He was really a nice guy, but he was older then me.

Well, I finally got up the nerve to call Harrison, and I was hoping he didn't refuse my offer. I asked Thomas for Harrison's phone number, and took a deep breath. When he answered, I told him who I was and asked, "Would you like to go see a movie?" He accepted, and it turned out that he lived on the campus at TSU.

He probably didn't think much of me, and I'm sure he had someone special in his life. He was from a close family and sometimes we would go over to his mother's house after church and eat her good cooking. She made full course meals and cakes and pies too. All of his sisters and brothers would be there. He came from a family of nine siblings and they all were good looking people. Their mother, a preacher, was a good God-fearing woman. Being a family person, I really liked being around people like Harrison and his family.

My cousin and her husband dropped me off at his place. When I knocked on the door, he opened it, came out, and we left. We decided to go to a late movie so Harrison bought the tickets from the Shamrock Theater for a 10:00 p.m. showing. He then took me to Hermann Park so that we could be alone and get to know each other better. This was the first time we were alone, and I liked it a lot. He asked me about my family, and I told him about my sisters, my parents, and the reason why I was in Houston to begin with. I noticed when I talked to him, he stared at me with trusting eyes. I couldn't believe how nice he was. It felt like I'd known him all my life.

Then I told him about my boyfriend. I thought I noticed something in his eyes, maybe disappointment. I asked him, "Are you dating anyone?"

He replied, "I don't have a girlfriend, but I do go out every once and a while. Being in law school keeps me busy."

I learned later that he was also the president of the Student Bar Association. This was a smart guy.

After talking in the cool Houston night, we headed back to the Shamrock Theater on Main to see the movie we both wanted to see. It was "48 Hours" staring Eddie Murphy. I noticed that Harrison was taller this night. I looked at his feet and saw cowboy boots. I never went out with a guy wearing cowboy boots. It must be a Houston thang.

During the movie, maybe in the middle of it, our arms touched as we shared the same armrest. There was something I felt just from that touch. I already liked him just from our conversation at the park. He had a lot of things about him that most guys I dated didn't have. He had a beard and naturally curly coal black hair. He was smart, but he was not my age. I was eighteen, and he was twenty-seven.

70

The next thing I knew, he was holding my hand. Then he gently kissed the tip of my index finger. All I thought was, *WOW*, and what I felt was this warm and tingly feeling in my abdomen. I looked at him shyly with a smile. We held hands the rest of the movie and afterwards. I didn't want this evening to end, and it didn't. He invited me to his place.

On the way there, while stopping at a red light, Harrison asked, "May I have a quick kiss?"

I replied teasingly, "My kisses will cause you to get dizzy, and you might wreck the car."

He laughed and said, "Maybe later, then. That would be nice."

I said, "Maybe, maybe not."

Being with him at that moment didn't make me feel so young. I felt comfortable with him, he was easy for me to like.

Once we were at his place, he invited me in. When I walked in, I heard soft music playing. It was the quiet storm on Magic 102 on the FM radio dial. He turned on a dim light and offered me a soft drink. As I sipped it, we talked some more with him sitting in a chair across from me. When I put the empty glass down, he walked over to me and took my hand. I stood and felt myself melt in his arms.

We moved slowly to a love song, and I rested my head on his shoulder. He smelled so good. I just hadn't felt this way with any other man. This was my first dance with a grown man. I only dated boys in the past. This was chemistry between two people. I felt warm all over. I felt so safe in this man's arms. Then we kissed, *WOW, make it last forever,* I thought. I didn't want this night to end.

We walked to his neatly made bed and shared more kisses, and he held me in his arms until I feel asleep. He took me back to my cousin apartment early the next morning—about 2:00 a.m. We kissed again and said goodbye.

When my cousin told me the next morning that the guy who was supposed to take me out had called while I was out with Harrison, I didn't care, and what Harrison and I shared the night before told me in my heart that I didn't care about my boyfriend either. My heart was feeling Harrison. I soon broke up with my boyfriend, and Harrison and I became closer. He was so sweet that I decided at the age of eighteen that he would be my one and only.

I guess it was those beautiful poems he wrote me when I took a trip to Florida with my cousin and her husband that made me know I loved him. He had written one for every day we were apart. That's when I knew he was my honey. After being a couple for three months, Harrison asked me to pick a date in that same year so that we could be married. I didn't think about the fact that Gilda and Thomas were the only people in my family who knew Harrison. That just didn't matter when I picked the date, August 6, 1983. The only thing that mattered was that we were in love. And I knew that without a shadow of a doubt.

Things were going so fast to me, and I still had not decided what I wanted to do with myself regarding my education. I only had a high school diploma. Harrison was a graduate of law school, and now he was planning to take the bar examination to practice law in Texas.

When August rolled around, we had a private wedding ceremony at his former pastor's home with the pastor's wife, my Cousin Gilda, and her husband, Thomas, present.

We exchanged our wedding vows. Gilda took pictures. It was so nice, so right for our relationship. We celebrated 23 years of marriage in August 2006, and plan to renew our wedding vows on our 25th wedding anniversary if it is God's will. We have five wonderful children, Kelley (22), Dominique (19), Harrison, Jr. (16), Jacob (11), and Joshua (18 months).

After all these years, he still makes me warm all over. So you see, we were meant to be together, a high school graduate from Miami, Florida, and a law student from Houston, Texas, with nothing in common but love. Well, that's how I met my sweetheart, and our love continues today as one.

<u>About the Author</u>

Sherille Fisher was raised and educated in Miami, Florida. She is the second of four daughters born to Johnny and Wilhelmina Williams. After living in Houston, Texas, since her arrival in 1983, she and her family moved to Tallahassee, Florida, in 2000. They lived there five years and in 2005, they returned to Houston.

Currently, she resides in Houston with her husband, attorney Harrison Fisher, Sr., and their five children. Although she has worked as a Certified Nursing Assistant (CNA) for many years, she is now working full-time in retail. She is also working diligently on revising her first novel for publication titled *Courtney's Collage*.

E-mail: <u>fisherlawhrf@aol.com</u>

12.

OASIS

Shauna Stephens-Batts

Should've been in an American cinema class, but I wasn't. Found myself at the *Oasis* with a hotdog in hand and a raspberry smoothie on the way. I heard the laugh but was too engulfed in my thoughts. Everything was on my mind. School. Work. All the men who had *done me wrong*.

The laugh…again…this time it caught my attention. I knew the laugh. The way it began in the pit of the stomach, churning and rolling, until finally releasing into air causing heads to turn. My head was the only one to remain in that direction.

"Excuse me. Miss, here is your smoothie."

I thanked the woman standing behind the counter and started in his direction. It was his eyes I noticed first. The way sparkles of sunlight danced in his pupils turning his brown eyes into pots of honey.

Think fast, Shauna. Think…fast…his name. Mario? Demarreio? Just yell out what comes to heart.

"Demarreio?"

There was no turning back now. In an oasis of confusion, college students rushing to and fro, I spoke his name. Of course, I knew him, but then again it had been years since I had actually called his name. His eyes lit up when he saw me.

"Shauna?"

He grabbed me in a warm embrace. Like a long lost relative. Not the kind of hug I was expecting. I wanted him to grab me, spin me around in the thin air, and plant a long passionate kiss

74

on my lips. Then stand me back on my two feet. I would be wavering in the wind because his kiss had been just that powerful. But the hug was warm, and it felt very good to be hugged like that.

I reminisced, thinking about how we met at Horace Mann Middle School. He was friendly to any and every one who would listen. I listened. We became friends. Early in the mornings we would stand in front of the school and chat. We played, dashing around the schoolyard with all of our friends.

At twenty-one he resembled nothing of the eleven-year-old boy I had met at Horace Mann Middle School. That eleven-year-old boy was nothing more than a mere existence in my *fast behind, lip gloss wearing, finger snapping, think I know everything but don't really know nothing* eleven-year-old world.

He was not one of the boys who I daydreamed about. He wasn't one of the "bad boys" who skipped school and cussed the teacher out. I only liked the boys with the "bad boy" image. He didn't fit into that category.

He was one of the "good boys," someone who was going to amount to something. Demarreio was one of the kids who had classes in the new part of school, worked from the new books, and did homework on the computers that actually worked. He was what anyone would call a "nerd."

They say that *age ain't nothing but a number*, but I refused to believe that. Age was everything. It was anything you wanted it to be. In ten years, *age* had really matured Demarreio.

He was five-foot-eleven, his skin the color of butterscotch. The smile he wore on his face caused his lips to curl up at the ends. He had beautiful lips. No one could smile the way he smiled. His hair was cut close to his scalp showing off his dark waves.

He was dressed in jeans, a polo, and Timberland boots which gave him a little edge of charm, but read that he was all man. The Timberland boots would later become his trademark.

What made me think he was different? Why was I going crazy over a guy who I had known for ten years?

I had never looked at him with such a critical eye. I got the feeling that fate was playing a dirty trick on me just to get me to understand *love*. Fate was appearing everywhere. *She* showed up one night at the Youth Fair. *She* followed me to the store. Now *she* was showing up at the place I least expected *her*...Florida International University. Just my luck!

We exchanged numbers. I promised to call at ten o'clock that night. It would be my lunch break at work. He told me he would wait by the phone for my call. He said that he waited ...waited...waited...for what seemed like an eternity. I called at 10:47 p.m.

"I thought you lied," he began as soon as he realized who was on the line.

"I have no reason to lie. I told you I would call, and I called." I giggled.

He laughed the laugh of a million smiles.

Right then and there, I think he realized I was not a part of the norm. My tongue was dangerous. If he started, I was sure to finish. It intrigued him. Added to my beauty. Charm. He called it *authenticity*. I was real and he had probably never dated anyone like me.

He, on the other hand, was the one I wanted to take home to mama. Mama would approve of this one especially after he doted upon her and asked for her blessing in dating me.

It wasn't long before we were an official couple. The phone calls from other guys stopped coming. There was no one else I wanted to know. I delve deep into his world, getting to know as much as I could. I met the family; he met mine. I invited him to church. He declined. He had never been asked before.

We enjoyed family outings together. This was new for him, but the love was unmistakably there. Love had found Shauna.

"What do you want from love?" he asked one rainy Sunday. I looked into the eyes I first noticed only months ago. My eyes studied his nose that from a distance seemed too big, but spoke wonders about his African ancestry. *Love*? I wanted to shout that word at the top of my lungs. *Love*?

I shrugged my shoulders. He asked again. And again. I began to cry. I looked into his eyes. *I know you've been hurt*. I looked into his hands. *Trust me*. I watched his chest heave in and out. *Believe in me*. He twiddled his thumbs waiting on an answer.

Everything. I wanted everything.

I wanted all of the things my mother never had. I wanted love to be everything that I dreamed about. Every waking moment of sheer bliss. I wanted love to hurt. I wanted love to cry. To be there when I needed it the most. Love needed to be able to pamper me. To put up with my mood swings. Love needed to know that I never meant any harm and that if you were patient enough, I would give one-hundred percent.

"Everything. I want everything."

He felt where I was coming from. That is when I knew for sure that I loved him. I wanted to marry this man. He was going to be the father of my children. Yes, yes, yes, Mr. Batts was the one. It was like a revelation.

All that time, I had been looking for love in all the wrong places. Love kept smacking me in the face, and I never saw her. Then one day, I decided to open my eyes and see what had been right there in front of my eyes for the longest.

He was a complex man. His heart had been broken too. I wanted to know who could break his heart. He was genuine. Pure.

Another woman?

Kinda.

Well, who?

People in general.

Would I be a part of the *people in general*? I didn't want to break his heart. I was scared. Scared that I would fall out of love as quickly as I fell in. Scared that in a moment's eye, I would be with someone else who proclaimed their love for me. Or seemed sincere.

Part of me didn't want him to hurt anymore. The other part was uncertain. I too had been scorned by love. But his scorn was of a different nature. His hurt stemmed from disappointments... neglect, he called it. Never did he say *regret*. They were learning experiences, and he didn't want his heart to hurt anymore.

I held his hand. He pulled away. *You don't understand Shauna. You don't want my baggage. It's too much.*

But I did want his baggage. I wanted to hurt as bad as he hurt so he didn't have to hurt alone. I wanted to cry when he cried, so he didn't have to cry alone. I wanted to carry the baggage because I didn't want him to carry the baggage alone. Good people often do more hurting than anyone else.

People took his kindness as a weakness. He wasn't weak. Caring, but never weak. Understanding…not weak. Slow to anger.

You could probably look up the word *nice* in a thesaurus and his picture would be staring back at you. This was my Dee.

Maturing into love was a difficult task for the both of us. We knew whatever we felt was love. It had to be love. What else could have me anticipating his every call?

I wanted to be near him 24/7. I wanted to drink his bath water. No one could tell me different. We grew together emotionally and physically. Before we knew what happened we were the proud parents of a baby girl.

She was our love child. We were young and in love. Now we had a child. She was our joy. Baby girl taught us how to love in a unique way. She gave us hope for the future.

It wasn't a perfect love, but I remember him telling me to trust him. I did. We went through happy moments and disappointments. Shedding tears seemed natural. *Uncertainty? Is this what we wanted?* He cried. *Uncertainty?* I cried.

We found out we were so different. But wasn't that what ultimately attracted us to each other? We were different. Raised with different ideals and beliefs.

I could hear mama saying, "True love can withstand any obstacle." She was right. Opposites attract and here we were doing what ninety-seven percent of people everywhere had done. *Giving up.*

I could not have been so wrong about the whole situation. All the time we were dating, I failed to look out for us. Instead I was concerned about my own feelings. My own needs. I fought to keep us together. We needed to survive.

I remembered the night I ran into him at the Youth Fair. He asked for my telephone number. Called for two straight weeks. Me saying that I had a man. Not really wanting to deal with his kind. He was too nice.

Fighting the urge to cry, I thought about the second year I ran into him at the store. Me saying that I was going to keep in touch this time. I never did.

Our meeting at F.I.U. was an epiphany. That was the eye-opener...revelation. He needed me in his life. I needed him. We needed each other.

When all was said and done we made a model couple. Being together for six years has been adventurous. Sort of like holding your breath under water and then coming up for air every once in a while. Everyday there was a surprise waiting for me.

Marry me? Be my husband. Isn't the man supposed to ask? I guess, but you're taking too long. Just want everything to be right. Everything is right. Don't need riches. Don't need a whole bunch of material things. Just want you and me. Let's do it.

Our engagement wasn't the customary means of becoming engaged. He never got down on one knee in front of a mob in a restaurant. I didn't need all of that. I just wanted him in my life forever. Forever seemed like a very long time, but I wanted him forever. He agreed.

Shopping for a ring was the hardest item on the list. He wanted a diamond that cost thousands of dollars. I wanted a ring of simple gold with a small, elegant diamond. I was never impressed by expensive jewelry. He wanted me to have the best. I already had the best.

In five months, the wedding was planned. We vowed to be together in a wedding ceremony on July 31, 2004. What we worked so hard for was now finally complete. He stared into my eyes and I said, "I do." I trusted him to make me feel like the queen I knew I was. He was my king.

As I declared my love in front of 200 people, I realized that in Demarreio's arms was where I always wanted to be.

I didn't have the hot dog in hand nor was I waiting for the raspberry smoothie I loved so much. Instead I was dressed in my wedding gown with smiling faces wishing us well.

Right then...

At that very moment...

I knew I would have an eternity to greet the sparkles of sunlight that danced in his pupils turning his brown eyes into pots of honey.

About the Author

Shauna Stephens-Batts currently resides in Miami, Florida where she has lived her entire life. She is happily married and the mother of two beautiful daughters, Iyaari and Sanaa. She currently teaches Language Arts to 7th grade students in the predominantly Spanish-speaking neighborhood of Hialeah which is located in Miami.

"Writing," she says, "is second to breathing. I need it to survive." She holds a Bachelor of Arts degree in English Literature from Florida International University and a Master of Science degree in Exceptional Student Education from Barry University.

In her spare time, Shauna loves writing poetry and short stories. She also enjoys singing in her church choir and spending time with her family. She is currently working on a collection of short stories.

Blog: www.sbatts.blogspot.com

E-mail: iyaari01@bellsouth.net

13.

RUNNING AWAY

H. Renay Anderson

Linda pushed the door open to reveal the sounds of music, conversation, and loud laughter. The bartender was making a ringing sound with the glasses he held in his hand. He was preparing drinks for customers just as fast as they were ordering them. Folks were dressed up in their best clothes and all seemed to be having a good time after a long work week. Linda and I walked in, passed the bar, and went straight up the stairs. We both could see that the club was as crowded as it always was on a Saturday night, both upstairs and downstairs. We wanted to sit by the dance floor, but there were no tables available. Then we spotted a table right next to the pathway where folks would be coming up and going down the stairs.

"Girl, I am going downstairs to get a drink from the bar. Do you want to come with me?" asked Linda.

"No, I am going to go sit down for a while. I am really tired. I put in ten hours today at work, and I am kind of mad about it because I was only supposed to work four hours this Saturday."

"Well, you just sit yourself on down and I will bring you a drink back."

"Thanks."

"Hey, come here first. Are my eyes red? Maybe I should go to the bathroom?"

"You look fine!"

"I'll be right back."

I sat at the table right next to the banister that led to the staircase that spiraled down into the bar area of P. J.'s Night Club. I was observing the room with nothing particular on my mind. It felt so good to be off work for a few days and just listen to some good music. I was five-foot-eight inches tall and in very good shape to be the mother of three children. After my separation from my husband, I had been through some really tough times financially. Now I had a good job and a great new apartment for me and my kids to live in. The apartment was close to schools and right next to Highway 280. San Jose had really grown since I moved here five years ago from the Bay Area of Northern California. I was finally living the life that I deserved.

I wonder what's taking Linda so long to come back with the drinks. She must have run into someone she knew downstairs.

Just then, I noticed a guy staring at me from another table. He smiled when he saw that he had my attention. *Oh no, he is cute, but he looks like he is a playa. I do not want another child to take care of who sits on his butt all day while I handle everything in the house!*

"Here's your drink," said Linda.

"What took you so long to come back?"

"I ran into Jessie, and he was running his mouth about the same old thing."

"You know you want to get back with Jessie."

"Honey, please stop me if you ever see me getting on that flight again."

"Whew, girl he was a trip, wasn't he? I'm surprised he would even want to be bothered with you any longer after you threw his freshly laundered clothes all over the street! Then to make matters worse, a city bus ran all over them!"

"I hate to say this Renay, but some men like women who 'sit horses with them' as my grandmother used to say."

"Now what does that mean?"

What she was talking about was a woman who confronts a man whenever she catches him in the act of doing wrong. The type of man who likes that in a woman may not ever tell the woman that, but he always comes back for more because he appreciates her not letting him take her for granted.

"I see you have an admirer." Linda observed, swiftly changing the subject.

"Hmmm, yeah he has been staring over here ever since you were downstairs. I don't like the way he looks."

"Why not, he looks mighty fine from over here."

"He looks sneaky to me."

"Well, girl, let's just finish our drinks and try to have a good time."

As the night went on, Linda and I danced with a few guys and chatted with some other lady friends who stopped by the table. All the while the mysterious guy at the other table kept staring at me, and I was starting to stare back at him. *Am I starting to feel attracted to this guy?* I didn't dare tell Linda because that would be speaking it out loud which would mean YES!

"All right, let's get out of here. The lights are starting to come up, and the D.J. is packing up his things."

"I am going to stop and holler at Jessie for a minute," said Linda.

"See there I told you, you wanted Jessie back."

"Nothing else exciting happened tonight. I might as well let him give me a few compliments before I go home to sleep by myself."

"Then give me the keys so I won't be standing around by myself looking like a sick monkey."

"Here you go," said Linda, while laughing.

Linda got up from the table and I started to gather my things together when I saw the mysterious guy out of the corner of my eye heading towards me. Before he could reach the table I jumped up and bolted towards the staircase and descended taking two steps at a time. I waved to Linda and pushed the door open and ran outside. I turned to look behind me and I could see the guy coming down the stairs through the tinted glass on the night club door. I turned and started walking towards the car very quickly. I did not know why I was running, but there was something warning me not to get involved with this guy. My life was perfect right now, and I didn't want to complicate it with a relationship.

When I made it to the car, I tried to put the key in the car door, but it did not fit. "Oh no, she gave me the wrong key!"

Just then, I heard a low sexy voice ask, "Do you need any help?"

"No, I am fine," I said, nervously. "My friend is coming right now. She accidentally gave me the wrong key to her car door."

"Can I stand here and talk to you until she gets here?" I really did not want him to, but I didn't want to stand there all alone.

"Sure that would be O.K."

"My name is Kenneth."

"My name is Renay."

"So Ms. Renay, do you live here in San Jose?"

"Yes, I have been here for a while. What about you, where do you live?"

"Oh, I am from North Carolina. I am just here working for a month for my job."

"Oh really?" I said.

Suddenly, the attraction to Kenneth started to surface. My mom and aunties were always talking about southern men. "Girl, you can give me a country man any day of the week!" my Aunt Camille would say. I started looking at Kenneth from his head to his toes and then back up again. I could see his mouth moving, but I hadn't heard a word since he told me where he was from. Kenneth was about three inches taller than me and had broad shoulders and big thighs just the way I liked them. He sported a mustache and a neatly groomed beard. He did not have on a suit like most of the guys in the club that night, but he did look mighty good in his black slacks and cocoa brown dress shirt.

"Renay, I can see your friend walking this way."

"Oh really?" I said, disappointedly. "How long are you going to be in town?" I asked.

"Just for a few more weeks then I am going back home. Why do you ask?"

"I was just wondering if you were getting to see everything that the San Jose area has to offer visitors.

"Well, I don't know. Is there something else I need to see?" he asked with a short sweet smile on his face. Before I could answer, Linda was at the car.

"Linda, this is Kenneth. Kenneth, this is Linda."

"It is nice to meet you, Kenneth."

"Same here," he replied.

Linda smiled at me then took the keys from my hand, opened up the car door, and got in. "Well, it seems like those are the right keys for the car door after all," said Kenneth with a grin.

"Yep," I said, embarrassingly. Changing the subject I said, "It was nice meeting you, Kenneth. I hope you enjoy the rest of your stay in San Jose."

"Nice meeting you also, Renay."

As Kenneth turned to walk away, I blurted out the question, "Would you like my telephone number?"

Kenneth turned around very slowly and walked back towards me. When he got close to me, he looked up, and smiled revealing the sexiest dimples I had ever seen on a man in my life!

"Yes, ma'am, I would love to have your telephone number."

And that's how I met my sweetheart while I was running away from love. We went on to share several years together.

About the Author

H. Renay Anderson is a widow, and the mother of three sons, who resides in Texas. She has a M.A. in Organizational Management and a B.S. in Management/Marketing. Her first book was titled: *Why Women Wear Shoes They Know Will Eventually Hurt Their Feet (2003)*. In 2005 she won a National AD contest for AD Candy.

In 2006, her short story, *Walking Through the Lessons of Life* was published in *Chicken Soup for the African American Woman's Soul*. She reviews books for Bella Online, EuroReviews, and BBW Reviews.

She has always had an interest in writing and expressing herself creatively. Even as a child she wrote poetry and often gave her poems to family and friends as gifts.

E-mail: renay6331@yahoo.com

Website: http://clix.to/renay

14.

SIMPLY LOVE

April McDermid

My parents divorced when I was young. My dad felt that marriage was equivalent to tying yourself to an anchor and jumping in the lake. In my struggle to find the right man, I slowly began accepting my dad's perception of love. I decided that I would marry when I turned ninety-years-old. That way, I reasoned, if I got sick of my husband—which I surely would—it wouldn't matter because he or I would die soon and we would be rid of each other. Each guy I met I would explain my theory much to their relief or disdain, depending on how serious their feelings were for me. None of the relationships lasted long, including the one I was in when I met the man who changed my mind.

I ended up in the beautiful state of Florida after running away from a bad relationship, a poisonous, potentially lethal one; and getting out of town seemed to be the favorable option. I had never heard of Lakeland before, but it was miles from where I came from so it was exactly what I was looking for. What I didn't know at the time was that I would fall in love twice, deep, strong, and true. First with Florida (I had a wonderful year exploring and enjoying my new home, the Sunshine State); and then with Scott.

We met at the limousine company where we both worked. Or rather, I worked. He had picked up his last paycheck when I had just begun at the company. I clearly remember the first time that I saw him:

Six-foot-seven inches tall, the strawberry-blonde-haired, blue-eyed man walked into the office of the limo company where I had just begun working. His immense frame filled the entryway. He was gorgeous!

"Hello," he casually stated giving me no impression that he had any idea that his very presence raised my blood pressure.

I smiled at him and turned back to the computer screen before he saw the pink flash across my cheeks. I knew it was there, I could feel my head getting hotter.

"Hello, you here to see Joanie? She's not here anymore. Moved back to Chicago," the boss answered and chuckled.

"Now you know I was just trying to help the poor girl out. She said she needed a ride to Wal-mart. I gave her a ride. That's it."

Joanie was the woman who had hired me. She was extremely everything, nice, large, and loud. She was not a subtle person. I learned later that one of his co-workers saw Joanie in his truck and had been harassing him about it since.

"She sure was fond of you," the boss said again chuckling.

"She's a nice girl, but not my type. Now her, on the other hand," he began.

I turned to see why he had paused. He was looking straight at me.

"Anytime, anywhere, and with a quickness," he finished.

If I thought my cheeks had colored before, it was not near to what happened then. I could hear the echo of my heart pumping, my head seemed full of blood, and my cheeks had to have turned a very embarrassing shade of scarlet. Again, I looked away and pretended that I was busy typing. Then he took his check and left.

"He sure likes you." I nodded.

"Who is he?" I asked.

"One of the drivers."

"Is he new? I haven't seen him before."

"No, he doesn't cover many runs. He's a paramedic, just drives part time. He just came in to pick up a check."

"Oh," I said. I noticed that he didn't give me his name but thought that if I asked for it again, he would know I was interested in the driver. I didn't want the boss to know that I was interested in a driver, even if he was just a part-timer.

It wasn't a new concept for the office girls to get hit on by the drivers and various other men who came through the limo company's doors. I've had many offers for dates in degrees varying from polite to crass and turned them all down. I wasn't sure what to do about this, though. He didn't actually ask me out; he just bluntly conveyed his interest and walked away without waiting for my response. Not that I would've known how to respond, my brain was too busy focusing on my awkward inward response to his presence and trying to hide my newly rosy cheeks and sweaty palms, and listening to the blood pump through my entire body to even consider forming intelligible words, let alone a whole sentence.

One week, seven slow days later, Mr. Gorgeous stopped in again. I was alone in the office working overtime, hoping to finish so that I wouldn't have to spend the rest of my weekend struggling to balance out the accounts that the previous girl had left behind.

"Hello." There again was that calm, friendly voice. My insides were slowly liquefying. A warm melted chocolate feeling gushed over me.

"Hello," I replied.

"Did Jerry leave an envelope for me?"

"Mmm. I don't know. Hold on a sec," I answered and headed to the desk.

"No, I don't see one."

"Ok. He said he'd have it for me on Monday, but I was passing through so I thought I'd check in anyway. I'll be working Monday, so I'll have to pick it up on my way through later in the week."

"All right, sorry about that," I said but didn't know why.

"It's ok. No big deal. I was just heading out for fancy coffee at the mall. I thought it would save me some time if it was ready for me."

There was a pause in the conversation. It was my turn to say something.

"Fancy coffee," I asked a little slow in my response.

"Yeah. I like Barney's coffee."

"Oh, I've never had fancy coffee before," I said and smiled up at him. At that moment, I realized that I wanted an invitation out for fancy coffee with this man.

You can't leave now you have too much work to get done. My mind was weighing the options, anticipating an invitation. I didn't want to say no, but if I said yes, I would be stuck working all weekend. Being invited would leave an opening for another chance later and that was a promising thought!

"Yeah, well that's where I'm going. Will you tell Jerry that I stopped by?"

Shot down. Well, at least I didn't have to worry about sitting in the office for the next two days.

"Sure," I said. "What's the name?"

"Scott McDermid."

"How do you spell that?"

"M-C-D-E-R-M-I-D."

"Oh, just like it sounds." I wrote it down and watched him walk out the door.

The warm gooey liquid that had covered my insides solidified and cooled. My heart slowed down and my shoulders drooped. Disappointed, I locked up and went home.

I learned later that he drove five minutes down the road before he realized that he'd missed the perfect opportunity to ask me to accompany him. He turned around in a construction zone amid a group of impatient drivers and an annoyed construction crew to return and find the office empty.

It took another week before I had gotten up the courage to call him. After searching through the employee files, I found his phone number and quickly wrote it down before heading home. I kept that phone number in my hand all evening contemplating when I should call, if I should call, and what I would say if I did call.

The following afternoon, I pulled out the paper and picked up the phone. *Please answer.* I thought. *No, don't answer.* Ring one. *Please don't answer. Please have an answering machine.* Ring two. *What should I say on the machine? Ok, please answer. Please.* Ring three. I took a deep breath. *Don't hang up. You have to do this.* Ring four. I willed myself to stay on the line. I had made it this far, only a few more seconds and it would all be over.

"Hello. You have reached Scott McDermid. I am not home right now, please leave a message."

"Hello, Scott. This is April from work. Please give me a call back when you get a chance. I'm not calling about work. My phone number is XXX-XXXX. Thanks. Bye."

I was convinced at the time that that was the stupidest message I had ever left on anyone's machine. It certainly wasn't clever. Now we both agree that it was the most important phone call I had ever made. Years later when I told him how nervous I was to make that phone call he told me that the second he heard my voice, he couldn't get to the phone and dial my number fast enough!

He called me back that same day. I have no idea how long we talked, but the conversation ended with an invitation to dinner the following Friday. Finally!

Right after I hung up the phone with Scott securing our first date, I called my boyfriend to let him know. I was not out seeking other relationships in any way. Having a boyfriend actually gave me an easy out when others would hit on me, but I couldn't name nor rid myself of the calm feeling that came over me the moment I met Scott. It would continue to grow stronger each time we talked until I no longer felt the rise of my pulse, or the sweat on my palms, but rather a complete sense of well being and serenity.

Friday came. Scott picked me up and I rode with him to St. Pete. We went to Hopp's for dinner. He ordered something with mushrooms and offered me one off of his fork. I was surprised. I wasn't a big fan of mushrooms, but I ate it anyway. Gagging in the middle of dinner on a first date did not seem very appealing, but I didn't want to appear standoffish. Thankfully, it tasted better than I anticipated. I didn't have to force it down my throat.

After dinner, we drove out to a nearby beach to find the front entrance blocked.

"The beach is closed until daylight," the older woman in the booth told us.

"We can't get in to just walk the sand?" Scott asked.

"No, I'm sorry," she answered.

"We won't make a mess of it, I promise. This is our first date, and we drove two hours just to get here." He smiled at the woman.

She smiled back.

"Ok, I'll open the gate, but don't cause any trouble."

"Thank you. We won't. We promise."

We walked along the beach for hours. The sand felt cool under my feet. I was walking beside the most perfect man I had ever met. We sat at a picnic table and talked the whole night as the evening grew cooler and the waves steadily flowed across the sand, and then retreated in a soothing rhythmic pattern that seemed to be only for our benefit.

On the ride home, I fell asleep. I awoke, surprised to find myself in my driveway. He walked me to the door and waited until he heard the click of the lock from the other side before leaving. Our first kiss would come later.

After our first date, our time together was a blur. I wanted to be near him as much as possible. A paramedic's schedule didn't allow nearly the free time I wanted to spend with him, neither did my work schedule. We spent most of our free time together. It was the first time in my life that I looked forward to seeing somebody so much. Seven years and counting and I still feel that way. We bask in each moment we get to sneak away from the rest of the world.

Our courtship lasted a total of two weeks. In that time, I had been introduced to real home country cooking (he talked his friend's girlfriend into cooking us a special dinner); met most of his friends, and many of his coworkers. Rumor had it that bets were being made as to how soon until we would be hitched. We beat all the records. The soonest guess was a month.

The afternoon he proposed, I think both of us were shocked, and then even more so by my response. "Yes."

He told his partner the news the following day. Rob and his wife invited us over for a celebratory dinner and pointed out that we really needed to pick a date for the wedding.

"You're not really engaged if you don't have actual wedding plans," Tracy said.

Rob pulled out his guitar case and handed us a day-by-day calendar. We all sat around separating and folding each page then tossing them into the case. When we finished, Scott and I each pulled out a day.

"December 24th," I said.

"Tomorrow," Scott said.

We dismissed those dates and tossed the papers aside. The four of us sat around pulling out the rest of the holidays, near holidays, and family birthdays and anniversary dates, the entire months of February and March, and all Tuesdays, Wednesdays, and Thursdays.

"Now, before you pick this last date, are you sure that you are willing to stick with any date pulled out? If not, you can just choose any date you want, and we can throw all these pages away now. Promise that whatever date you pull out will become your anniversary," Rob said.

We both promised.

"Ok, pick a date."

Rob shook the brown case and ruffled up the papers one more time before sliding it over to me. I stuck my hand in sliding it through the tiny folded pages and gripped a hold of one. I handed it to Scott.

"Are you sure," he asked.

"Yes, are you?"

"Yes." He quickly unfolded it and handed it back to me.

"April 23rd," I announced.

We called our parents and told them to mark their calendars. The wedding ceremony would be held in Florida, but my grandmother had cancer. She couldn't miss her treatments so she had to stay in New York and would miss the ceremony. Worse, she still hadn't met Scott and wouldn't be able to prior to the date. I insisted that Scott meet her before the wedding. He agreed. We packed up and drove the twenty-four hour trip straight through so that he could meet the rest of my family.

He was greeted with open arms. My mother, grandmother, stepfather, aunts, and uncles all easily welcomed him into the family. Scott had won them all over as effortlessly as he had me.

I wasn't too surprised; he had won my loving, protective father over almost instantly. Scott had walked right up to my dad, introduced himself, and shook his hand. I saw the change in my dad's eyes, the surprise, and then the smile. I've dated guys before who have been introduced to my father, some have spent holidays with us, but none have made such a positive impression in such a brief moment as Scott had in those first two minutes.

We had a wonderful time in New York, and we soon decided that since the person I truly wanted to witness our wedding wouldn't be able to, maybe we could just do a secret wedding with my grandmother as a witness, and we could still keep the April 23rd ceremony for everybody else. Our scheme would've worked had my grandma not felt uncomfortable about keeping the secret from my mother.

Since the only way to have my grandma there was to also have my mother there, we had to tell the rest of the family. Scott called his mother to tell her the plan: we applied for our marriage license and had a two-day waiting period before we could be married before the local judge. His mother, having not yet met me, was understandably concerned and threw a tirade over the phone. She tried all means possible to change his mind, including trying to gain support from my mother and grandmother. After Scott got some reasonable advice from a wise third party who said, "You're not marrying your mother are you? You're promising to hold this woman above all others for the rest of your life, that includes your mother," we decided to get married by the judge.

In all of the excitement, we didn't realize that we had forgotten to tell my father of the change in plans until we were driving back to Florida. He still feigns surprise when we remind him that our anniversary is in February, not in April. We did try to balance it all out later. He was the first person Scott told when we learned I was pregnant. Everybody else received the news after my dad.

The moment Scott walked into that office, my life was changed. It was that very same instant that I felt that something that I have yet to find a better way to describe than simply love.

About the Author

April McDermid was born and raised in Upstate New York before moving to Central Florida. She relocated to Tallahassee almost four years ago when they learned that her husband's childhood home was abandoned and in foreclosure. She is a homemaker raising three children and has spent two years caring for her father who is recovering from a stroke he had while she was pregnant with her third child (who decided he couldn't wait to see his grandfather – he was delivered full term one floor up from where her father was being treated). The nurses would wheel her dad in to them and they spent their days recovering together. She believes grandchildren have amazing healing powers! Her dad worked hard to overcome his aphasia so that he could read afternoon stories to his grandbaby.

April and Scott have been married for seven fantastic years. On their wedding day, they promised each other a fiftieth anniversary. She is hoping to give this book to him as an anniversary gift in February.

E-mail: AMcDermid@comcast.net

15.

SWEET SUNDAY MORNING

Sylvia A. Thomas

On this particular Sunday morning, as I got myself ready for church, I did not realize that it would be in this Holy place, the Lord's house, that I would meet my soul mate, my sweetheart. But I did!

The details of that Sunday morning in church are hazy to me. I do not think that this man and I said any more then a casual 'hello' in church. At least, that's my story; however, I think that he made his heart and prayers for me known to God from the day we met. He had chosen his wife!

I did not take notice of this man until the youth night which happened sometime later. It was on his birthday. I, being new to the group, thought it would be nice if I gave this young man a nice birthday card. I was so embarrassed after he opened the card, smiled, and informed me that I had spelled his name incorrectly.

I am, by nature, a very shy person so it was difficult for me as I struggled to mingle with this new youth group that I had become a part of. It was particularly difficult to try to talk to this young, handsome, doting college student, whom I had no idea at the time, would steal my heart. I remember making causal conversation with him, but of course, everything was coming out wrong. Fortunately for me, everything I was saying was not coming out wrong to his ears.

This and subsequent casual meetings with this young gentleman began my husband's pursuit of me. From what he has told me, he prayed to God and made certain promises to God about me if the Lord would allow him to have me as his wife.

God did grant him his wish, for which I have been mightily blessed to have been the beneficiary of these prayers. I am blessed to have been chosen by a godly man who sought our Lord and Savior Jesus Christ for his wife. I have not ever regretted becoming this man's wife.

This wonderful man and I had a beautiful wedding with all of the sentiment and glamour that weddings create. He immediately whisked his new bride out of the mainland for a romantic honeymoon in Hawaii. These are memories that I will always cherish. In some ways, these memories serve as the glue to our marriage that helps hold it all together. We have now been married for over sixteen years by the grace of Almighty God.

Life has taken us through many twists and turns, however, with each step we climb, another brick is put in place. This man keeps proving over and over again that he truly is the knight in shining armor sent from God to me.

He is my Sweetheart!!

I have learned that we truly can meet the person whom God has for us but only on God's terms. For all of my single sisters, I say: "Let God send you your mate; Let your husband-to-be choose his wife."

Whoso findeth a wife findeth a good thing.
Proverbs 18:22

About the Author

Sylvia A. Thomas is the wife of Garry Thomas. They have five children and four grandchildren. Sylvia is an ordained minister and the owner of a real estate company.

She is also an accomplished writer of two published books entitled, *Me? Jewish? The Revelation of a Black American Christian Jewish Woman,* and her most recent publication, *Tough Skin.* She enjoys writing, reading, studying the Bible, and spending time with her family.

Email: SylviaThomasMinistries@yahoo.com

Website: www.NewIsraelOnline.org

16.

THE STEREO MAN

Francina Roberts-Cargile

Two years after moving to Lakeland, the kids and I found ourselves settled in a singlewide mobile home. It was new, very comfortable, and located in an excellent spot. We were living near the edge of town on open acreage that was spotted with orange and grapefruit trees. Gardens and pastureland were still visible from the main road, and the quiet was intoxicating.

In the spring, Kae, Mike, and I decided to plant a garden to develop their appreciation for fresh veggies. They would also enjoy romping through the sand and playing outdoors. There were several kids next door to keep them company, boys and a set of twin girls, who liked taking care of younger kids. I was still getting use to the idea of being a vibrant, young divorcee, and mother raising three babies on my own. But Kae and Mike were school age, and Jae was such a good baby, it was relatively easy.

I had regained my strength, my shape, and a desire to spruce up the house, so I examined my stereo to see if it would work. Realizing a need for music to help me through my spring-cleaning, I dropped everything to find a stereo repair shop when I discovered mine wouldn't play. I loaded up the car with the box and the kids and headed for the mall. Surely there would be a place to repair or replace it nearby. We needed to hear music.

Having no mechanical aptitude, I headed for the nearest department store to ask for help. They sent me around the corner and down the way to the stereo shop near the back of the mall. Since I was on a specific mission of stereo repair, I hadn't bothered to get dressed all pretty and slick. It was summer so the kids and I didn't change from our shorts and shirts we were wearing to clean house.

The shop we entered seemed upscale and expensive and the guy who bothered to wait on us was all dressed up in a suit. Well, it was of no consequence to me because I was on a mission.

"May I help you?" the man inquired.

"Yes!" I answered. "It won't work!" I added. "And I don't know what's wrong with it."

"Let me take it in the back and have a look," he said. To that, I happily obliged.

It took him a little while, but he finally returned and said, "I think you need a new needle, and we don't carry it." I was too disappointed. "I can tell you where to get it though." I was all smiles because I was still finding places in Lakeland.

He handed me the name of a shop I could take my box to then stopped to question me more. "By the way, do you live around here?"

"Yes," I answered.

"Well, where? I don't think I have seen you here before."

"On Providence Road." I said reluctantly.

"Is that right? I live near Providence Road also. So, just where on Providence Road do you live? It's a long road you know."

"Uh huh." I stalled.

"So, what's your phone number?" he asked.

"It's in the book." I quipped, knowing I hadn't divulged my name. I chuckled to myself walking out of the door.

"What kind of car are you driving?" he asked prodding for more info.

"A *red* one!" I replied, with emphasis on the color. I left the store because the last thing I wanted to do was meet a man. I wasn't dressed, wasn't in the mood, and didn't have the time.

Three weeks flew by and although I really wasn't looking for the guy, I did notice that he lied about stopping to visit. After all, he was the one to say he lived near us and wanted to stop by, so I surmised it was just a line he gave me. My job was swell, the kids were under control, and I was making decent money, so I let my hair down and began to live a little. I called my mom and asked her to come and spend the weekend so I could go out and have some fun with no worry about the kids. Mom complied and I got invited to an all night astrology charting party.

The party was a blast, and I didn't get home 'til 7:00 a.m. I was so tired, my eyes were red, and the make up I wore was smudged so I donned a gown and dove into the bed. Mom and the kids always had a ball cooking breakfast and doing the things that you love to do with only your Grandma.

Before I could fall into a deep sleep, there was a knock at the door. Mom answered and called to me, "Fran, there is someone here to see you!"

Half dazed, I stumbled to the door of my bedroom and received the shock of my life. It was the stereo man! Of all the days he could have stopped by he picked this one.

"Hi," I muttered. "I'm sorry, I have been up all night doing astrology charts so I am very tired."

"Really!" he smiled, all chipper and energetic. "Well, I'm on my way to Tampa, but I thought I would stop because this is the first time I've seen your car here." I smiled but inside I cracked up because that meant he had been looking and we weren't home. *Ha ha! That's a good thing!*

"So when is your birthday?' I asked.

"June 20, 1954," he said, as he walked out of the door. When I heard that I awakened immediately and completely. June 20th is also my birthday, and he was the second man I had met who was born on that day. I leaned out of the door and yelled, "Goodbye, see ya later!" *What a delight to meet another June 20th guy. This is going to be fun!*

Months went by this time and there was no sign of the stereo guy. So one day, I interrupted my conversation with the kids and announced we were going to the mall. We all got dressed and took off in the car and arrived at the mall just in time to meet a huge Saturday crowd. We were bending the corner when my eye caught sight of the stereo guy walking in the opposite direction. He was hugging some ugly, fat girl and grinning from ear to ear. He waved and smiled at us as he passed us by like we were no longer the ones he was chasing. This infuriated me because I had not been looking for him and the first time I took an active interest, this is what I find.

It didn't take me long to forget about my interest and I filled my days with work, kids, and family life. One morning when the kids and I were finishing breakfast, we heard a knock at the door. When I answered I saw the stereo guy standing on the step.

"Are you busy?" he asked.

"No," I said.

"Good," he added. "Can you follow me to the tire store?" *So what is he up to now*, I thought.

"I'd like to sit and talk with you while they work on my car."

"Oh!" I exclaimed, that made a little more sense of his request. So we loaded up the car and followed him there.

We waited in the car while he spoke to the attendant and he joined us shortly for the ride back to our house. I couldn't wait to hear what lie he would use to explain what he was doing all wrapped up in the mall.

As we sat in the living room the kids went out to play, and we were able to talk openly together. "I met someone else since I saw you in the mall."

"Oh, really?" I said with a tease in my voice.

"Yeah," he confirmed. "I like her a lot."

The nerve of this donkey! I thought. *How dare he tell me he met someone else! I will make him regret this!* I thought. So I listened to him talk and when his car was ready I was more than happy to get rid of him.

Well, I gave up on him because, after all, I wasn't looking for a man anyway. But this joker kept coming by every two or three weeks, and I tell you he could talk more than any five girls I knew. He was of no use to me, but he seemed to have a need to talk so I listened for much longer than I want to admit. I decided he had made me his friend regardless and that was the way I saw him for quite some time.

It was as if someone fast forwarded our friendship and now the stereo guy was stopping by between 5:00 and 8:00 o'clock, staying long enough to play with my kids, and then leaving. I wasn't sure what he was doing, but I thought, *Well, maybe, I'll just see where this leads.*

I watched Dwayne fall in love with Kae, Mike, and Jae. He had a natural affinity for children, and they seemed taken aback with an adult who liked to play. *What a crock!* I thought. Anyway I waited to see just how long this relationship would last and to my surprise it was genuine. It's real hard for any girl not to like a guy who falls in love with her kids, so this may be where the playing field took on new importance.

All before his player Gemini twin was the one out front and center stage, so that's the twin I sent out to meet him. Now, I think for the first time, the more serious, family oriented twins were meeting and that brought to light a new agenda.

Our conversations became more down to earth and all about our personal aspirations. As time passed, we evolved beyond being good friends and became lovers as well. Humm…guess that was inevitable.

By this time, the pace stepped up and the time we spent together grew to the point where we were seldom apart. That was of great concern to me because I vowed never to live with a man who wasn't my husband. I wasn't sure just how committed this guy was to the kids and I, but I was about to find out. I approached the subject with him and discovered the idea of marriage and family was not foreign to him, but he really had to take some time in thought and prayer concerning the five of us.

He was not alone in his need for prayer and contemplation. This would be my second marriage, and I wanted to avoid prior mistakes. Although it seemed silly, I asked God to write my answer in the sky so I could be sure of his approval, but He reminded me that he had given us "free will" leaving me to decide for myself.

Well, that subject didn't surface again until 6:00 a.m. one Thanksgiving morning. My parents were coming for dinner and like older people, they got up before the chickens to drive from St. Petersburg to Lakeland. It was only fifty miles, but you know how it is when older folk aren't real sure of where they are traveling. They seem to want plenty of time to get lost and then find their way with help.

Needless to say, they arrived at my house long before we awakened including Dwayne. We were forced into answering some direct questions and my parents were prepared to sit until they got the right answer.

Thanksgiving dinner was wonderful; no one cooks like my mom. That meant that we were stuffed much like the turkey, and all we could do all afternoon was watch TV and groan. Dwayne ate and left to visit with his mom's family out in the country. I was the one who had to face my parents and speak to why we were ALL asleep when they arrived. My emotions jumped from compliance and talking to maybe it's none of your beeswax but it was my mom asking and you don't ignore your mother.

Later that evening when Dwayne returned, he said, "I have something to tell you."

So after the kids were asleep, we talked, and he admitted to me that for the first time he realized he didn't want to be without me. "I missed you while I was out in the country, and I want to marry you."

Well, I was wordless, but happy to hear the commitment. Once that issue was settled, there was no time to waste because we had a wedding to plan. Christmas vacation was coming up fast, and we couldn't think of a better time to double our excitement and happiness by getting married beside the Christmas tree. It took some doing but we managed to make a wedding gown and hang all of the stockings just in time!

We were married at 6:30 p.m. on December 29, 1977, and the rest of the story, as they say, is history! Ours is currently a marriage of twenty-nine years. Dwayne and I had two more beautiful baby girls. We were forced to strap on our roller skates just to stay two steps ahead of five multi-talented children. And we thought we had accomplished an amazing feat until the triplet grandchildren arrived!

About the Author

Francina Roberts-Cargile is a native of Gainesville, Florida. She grew up living in several Florida cities both large and small, which developed her love for country living, gardening, and southern cooking as well as the arts and cultural events. Ms. Cargile is a University of Florida graduate whose work as an occupational therapist was a perfect blend of two cherished subjects: arts/crafts and science. Ms. Cargile is currently retired but continues to enjoy singing, volunteer church work, and desktop publishing in her spare time.

She writes short stories as a tribute to having been married thirty years and raising five children. She boasts of surviving to talk about the numerous child-rearing adventures and anticipates publishing them in the near future.

E-mail: Nanfran@polaris.net

17.

WE'RE JUST FRIENDS

LaShaunda Carruth-Hoffman

In January, 1995, Clyde Hoffman walked into the room, and I completely forgot I was an engaged woman. I was mesmerized like the other women in the library meeting room. Gone was the tall lanky young man with the cute smile. In his place was a well built man with a sexy smile.

He came to the meeting for the ten year class reunion. I'd hoped to see him and three other guys who were my male friends in high school. Clyde and I had a couple of classes together, and we used to tease each other. I wasn't interested in Clyde as a boyfriend. Back then I was foolish enough to believe that you didn't date your friends. I later learn differently.

"Hi Clyde," I said.

He said, "Hi," and gave me a bear hug.

As we caught up with each other's lives, I found out we had spent time in the Navy. I'd been out a few years, and he'd just been discharged. As I watched him talk with our other classmates, I thought the Navy had done him well. He was all grown up with a great personality to go with it.

After the meeting, the reunion committee went out to eat, and I offered to drive Clyde to the restaurant. I tried to ignore the attraction I had for him. I was an engaged woman. My fiancé had joined the Army and was in basic training. I needed to concentrate on him, not on this old friend.

Ignoring my feelings worked for a while as I grew to know this older Clyde. He still liked to tease me, and he had a great sense of humor. He was so nice. I tried to fix him up with my friend. It didn't work. She met someone before the assigned date.

Clyde and I grew closer as we conversed over the telephone, and I took him on errands because he didn't have a car. My family fell hard for Clyde too. My sisters teased that I liked Clyde.

"No," I replied. "We're just friends."

"Yeah right," they laughed.

Once a month, our class reunion committee held different meetings and mingled at the local clubs. Each time I offered Clyde a ride to the events.

There were always one or more classmates hitting on Clyde. I tried to act like it didn't bother me, but inside I was seething. This confused me more. I had no right to be jealous or did I?

My growing feelings for Clyde made me realize I wasn't ready to become an Army wife. I broke off my engagement. Clyde was there to lend a shoulder to cry on. He let me know I did the right thing.

At the next event, everyone noticed I was no longer engaged. "Are you and Clyde dating?"

"No," I replied, "We're just friends."

I approached Clyde one afternoon, "Everyone thinks were dating."

Yeah," he said in his sexy tone.

"Maybe we should try it," I suggested.

"Why not," he agreed.

We went for ice cream and our love story began. On November 6, 1996, I became LaShaunda C. Hoffman. At our twentieth year class reunion, everyone said they knew we'd get married. This year we'll celebrate ten years of wedded bliss.

About the Author

LaShaunda Carruth-Hoffman is a happily married mother of three children who resides in Saint Louis, Missouri. She's also the editor/publisher of Shades of Romance Magazine, an award winning online magazine for readers and writers of multicultural literature.

Blog: www.lashaunda.blogspot.com
              http://sormag.blogspot.com

E-mail: sormag@yahoo.com

Website: http://sormag.com

18.

WILLING TO LOVE

Barbara Joe-Williams

I'd been in the military for almost a year when I first met my future husband. After graduating from Oak Grove High School in Rosston, Arkansas, as the valedictorian of my senior class, I joined the United States Navy. Knowing that I wasn't ready for college, I signed up with the Navy because I didn't want a job, I wanted an adventure that would provide me with room, board, and a steady paycheck. And what a glorious adventure it turned out to be. Not only did I meet my sweetheart on my first duty tour, but we got to travel overseas together before returning to the United States and starting college in the fall of 1983 in Tallahassee, Florida.

Before our first meeting, I had my entire life mapped out. I wasn't ready or willing to love anyone. I was going to make a twenty year career out of the military as a single woman, earn a college degree along the way, then retire at the end of my stint, and start a second career as a professional somebody. Yes, that was the plan that I had in my mind when I left home to attend six weeks of grueling basic training in Orlando, Florida, in the hot summer sun. I'd always dreamed of living in a warm climate year-round, but the Florida heat in full Navy dress uniform was almost unbearable.

The day we met, I was stationed at the Naval Air Station in Jacksonville, Florida, serving in the communications field as a newly enlisted service woman. I was working the evening shift where I reported to work at three o'clock and got off at eleven. On this particular springtime afternoon, I decided to walk to work early, wearing my casual dungaree uniform, and go to the cleaners first to drop-off a couple of sundresses. I draped them over my left arm, grabbed my black shoulder bag, and headed out the door at least an hour before my shift was supposed to begin.

The dry cleaners were on the opposite end of the base from the women's barracks and the communications center was in the middle somewhere. As I approached the intersection to the right of the communications building, I noticed a tall Marine, with dressed shirts draped over his right arm, stepping in my direction. My first reaction to his side view was, "Oh my God, there's a Marine walking towards me." I knew that if I kept walking at the pace that I was, we would meet on the right side of the building where I was employed. I couldn't really tell whether or not he was a handsome gentleman, but I could certainly tell that he was built. Standing at approximately six-foot-one, around a hundred-eighty pounds with a trim waist, and wearing his uniform with pride, he was the epitome of a serviceman. I also noticed the sergeant stripes on the side of his neatly pressed khaki shirt as his long strides quickly brought him closer to me.

With my cap pulled over my face blocking out the beaming sunlight, I barely turned to smile in his direction as he spoke to me when our paths finally crossed at the intersection. "Hi," I replied. "I guess we're headed to the same place," I joked, staring down at the clothes hanging across his right arm.

"Yeah, it looks like it," he answered keeping his eyes straight ahead.

"My name is Barbara Joe," I stated softly.

"I'm William," he replied without breaking his stride.

We made polite conversation as our steps fell into sync. Looking down at his glistening shoes, I could tell that he was what we often referred to as a real "gung ho" Marine. I was a little nervous as we walked past the base communications center making a straight path to the dry cleaners.

Trying to cover up my nervousness, I simply made light-hearted comments about the base to keep the conversation going. Drivers stared us down as they passed. I guess it was unusual to see a Marine and a Navy person walking around the base together. Most of the Marines stayed to themselves and were housed on a separate end of the base far away from the Navy personnel.

As we approached the cleaners in the distance, we asked each other very general questions about where we worked on base, commented about the weather, and tried to basically scope each other out on the sly. I admired the way that his uniform was fitting as we stepped together. I can still see the creases in the front of his khaki shirt, the red stripe down the side of his navy pants, and the spit shined black shoes that he wore. Oh yeah, I was breathing in everything about this strong stately looking man as we walked together on this warm day in the Florida sun. In an effort to divert my attention from him, I remember glancing around at the passing traffic and workers in the street as we continued our short journey to the cleaners. I didn't want him to see that I was truly enthralled with his sharp appearance.

I couldn't guess his age right away. Just the fact that he was a sergeant told me that he had to be at least a couple of years older than me. I'd joined the Navy right after high school, and I was still only eighteen years old. And my young heart was fluttering wildly as we marched in uniform to our own music.

Minutes later, we arrived at the dry cleaners. Upon entering the doorway, he removed his hat, turned to me, and flashed a perfectly aligned smile. I saw the kindest eyes that I'd ever seen in my life. Being an extremely shy person, he immediately looked downward as I stared at the side view of his gently smiling face. He stood holding the door for me until I slowly made it inside.

I could feel his eyes on my backside as I approached the counter with my sundresses still in tow. I proceeded to check in my clothes with him standing to the side. Being a mannerable young man, he let me check in my clothes first. Then, I stepped to the side and politely waited for him to do the same.

Apparently, there was a problem with the other clothes that he wanted to pick up. I can't remember the cause of the altercation, but I could tell that he was visibly disturbed that his clothes weren't ready for whatever reason.

"This won't take long," he said, smiling in my direction. I returned his smile with a nervous one of my own. I was hoping that this would be resolved quickly so that we could leave together.

I discretely checked my watch as he conversed with the laundry attendant. I had to be at work in a matter of minutes.

Although I didn't want to leave this stranger who I was immensely attracted to, I couldn't afford to be late for work because Uncle Sam didn't play like that.

"Ah, I have to get to work," I reluctantly stated when the attendant finally walked away. "It was really nice meeting you." I made eye contact with him and smiled as innocently as I could.

"Yeah, same here," he replied.

I held his eyes for a few seconds, slowly turned, and then walked back through the doorway. I could hear my heart pumping as I headed down the street to the base communications center.

Wondering if I'd ever see those brown eyes again, I punched in my security code, and headed to the back lounge to clock in. I didn't have a clue that I'd just met my future husband.

The next morning, I woke up in the barracks where I shared one room with two other women. It was around seven-thirty. Daylight was just breaking through as I heard my roommate's perky morning voice.

"Hey, B.J.," Connie blared. "I'm going to get up and head for the gym to play some basketball. Would you like to join me?" she asked, jumping out of bed. Connie and I had been together since we met in San Diego, California, at Radioman "A" School over a year before.

"No way, I worked late last night and then I had to walk all the way home. I'm still tired."

"Ah, come on. Let's go play for awhile, and then you can come home and sleep all day," she pleaded, rubbing her eyes. Her curly blonde hair was scattered all over her head as she stared at me, waiting for a response. We worked in the same facility and were often referred to as "salt and pepper."

"You must be out of your mind. I don't feel like playing no basketball today. I just worked the late shift while you were in a warm bed sleeping. Why don't you wake up Annette and ask her to go with you?" I jokingly asked, pointing to our other roommate with her head buried beneath the covers. It was a Saturday, and I knew that she normally slept all day on the weekend. There wasn't anyway that Annette was getting out of bed to go play basketball with Connie. So she continued to work on me thinking that I would eventually give in to her whining.

"Well, you're already awake, and I'm already up. So let's go play a couple of games or something and come on back. I promise you, we won't stay more than an hour. I might even let you win today," she replied, mockingly. By this time, she was standing in front of her locker at the foot of her middle bunk pulling on a pair of white athletic shorts and a t-shirt which was our favorite summer attire in 1980.

After thinking for a few seconds, I threw the covers back, and grudgingly replied, "Oh, alright. But we'd better be back here in an hour." Connie was fully aware that I loved the game of basketball, and it would be hard for me to turn down a challenge to play against her even though she didn't have much skill.

"That's great, I knew that you wouldn't let me down," she stated as I stumbled out of bed and quickly changed into my shorts, t-shirt, gym socks, and tennis shoes.

"Hey, I'm just walking with you over there so that I can tell you about this guy that I met yesterday," I stated, remembering the tall stranger with the sweet smile.

"Oh, so you met someone yesterday did you?" she asked, using her southern drawl. Connie was from somewhere in Missouri. She always bragged about being from the "Show Me" state.

"Yes, I did. And he's a Marine," I beamed.

"Oh goodness," she quickly replied, changing to a sour tune. "I sure hope that you don't get mixed up with a darn jar-head."

"See, you don't even know the guy, and you're calling him names. He seemed really nice," I stated defensively, and then proceeded to tell her about my afternoon encounter with the young jar-head.

A few minutes later, we were headed to the gym engaged in lively chatter. As we walked through the double glass doors, my eyes wandered to my left towards the weight room with a huge glass panel. Lying flat of his back on the weight bench was the Marine that I'd met the day before on my way to the dry cleaners. When my eyes landed on his sweaty muscular biceps, they stretched wide open, and my lower lip must have dropped down at least two inches. I was absolutely speechless for two seconds. I

113

couldn't believe that he was lying flat of his back right in front of me.

"B.J. what's wrong with you? Are you alright?" Connie asked, staring directly into my opened mouth. I pulled my lips together, batted my eyes, and swallowed hard.

"Yeah, I'm fine. That's—that's the guy that I was telling you about in there on the weight bench," I stated, nodding my head in that direction. At that moment, William looked up at me. When our eyes made direct contact, he sat up straight on the bench, and stared at me. I could tell immediately that he recognized me too.

Connie couldn't contain her surprise. "That's the Marine. Oh man, he's not bad looking, B.J. He's not bad looking at all," she repeated for good measure.

By the time that we made it to the doorway leading into the gym area, he was in front of me with his roommate, Harold, by his side. We introduced ourselves to each other again along with our roommates. A few minutes later, we were all laughing and playing a game of basketball together.

After beating us in a couple of basketball games, it was almost lunch time, and I was ready to head back to the barracks. William and his roommate escorted us to our room where we once again said good-bye to each other and went on our separate ways.

"Well, Connie, what do you think?" I asked, the second we entered the barracks.

"I think he's mighty shy for a Marine. I don't think that he said more than two words the whole time."

"Yeah, he seams to be on the quiet side, that's for sure."

"Considering how much you like to talk, that might be a good thing," she stated with a sly grin. I playfully slapped her on the arm as I headed for the shower. I knew that I was attracted to William, but I didn't have any idea how he felt about me at that time. I would soon learn that it was a mutual attraction. However, I still wasn't sure if I was willing to love him.

"Hey, B.J., you have a telephone call," one of my co-workers stated. As I made it back to the lounge area, I wondered who was calling me at work on a Monday afternoon as I picked up the telephone receiver and answered, "Hello."

"Hi, Barbara, this is William," he stated.

"Hello, William. How are you?"

"I'm doing fine. I hope that you don't mind me calling you at work, but I didn't know how else to get in touch with you."

"No, that's okay. I don't mind."

"Ah, I was just calling to say hello," he stated, and then fell silent.

"Well, it was nice of you to call, but I need to get back to work."

"Yeah, I know."

"Okay, I'll see you later."

"Would you like to go out with me sometime?" he blurted out. Since I didn't see that coming, it took me a second or two to respond.

"Well, I don't know. Are you asking me out?"

"Yes, I am."

"Let me have a number where I can reach you, and I'll call you back on my break," I replied, scrambling for a paper and pen.

The next hour felt like three long hours before I was caught up enough with my work to take a break. Rushing to the telephone, I pulled the paper out of my front pocket with the number that William had given me. After a few minutes of strained conversation, we agreed that he would pick me up on Saturday evening around six o'clock, and we'd go to dinner and then a movie.

I changed clothes at least five times the following Saturday afternoon. I finally decided to wear a two-piece tan colored outfit. The top had a v-neck with short sleeves and the long straight cut skirt had a deep walking slit on the left side. I struggled into a pair of chocolate pantyhose and buckled the ankle strap to my cognac-colored woven leather high heels. Both of my roommates were there helping me to get dressed as I fiddled back and forth between outfits and curling my jet black shoulder length relaxed hair. While they made their little jokes and snide remarks about me dating a jar-head, I kept my mind focused on other things like what type of car my sergeant would be arriving in.

Our room was adjacent to the back parking lot so that we'd have a clear view of his car when he drove up. Since he was walking when we first met, I hadn't bothered to ask William what

115

type of vehicle he would be driving. So I had my roommate, Annette, posted at the window to keep an eye out for any strange cars pulling in.

"Uh oh, I bet this is him," Annette stated, staring intensely through the large window. "I see a car that I've never seen before turning in here with a big black man behind the steering wheel." Rushing to her side, I peeped through the window to see my Prince Charming pulling up in a brown Ford Pinto station wagon. "Oh my God!" I exclaimed. "He's driving a Pinto!"

"Alright, it's a Ford! My daddy said that they make great cars!" Annette beamed with excitement.

I turned and looked at her thinking that she couldn't be serious, but then again, she was a country girl from Mobile, Alabama. Since none of us had a ride, and were tired of walking across base everyday, we eventually learned to love that brown Pinto station wagon.

I made one of them answer the door and ask William to wait in the lounging area while I pretended to finish getting ready. Moments later when I walked through the doorway, he stood like a perfect gentleman to greet me wearing a nice pair of brown dress trousers and a casual tan shirt. I instantly thought that he looked almost as good as he had in that uniform on the first day that we'd met.

Anyway, I hadn't worn heels in so long that I had to really concentrate on my walking especially since I didn't want to fall flat on my face. Somehow I made it through the parking lot in those heels knowing that my two roommates were watching every step that I took. Surprisingly, he opened the door on the passenger side for me and closed it after I slide around in my seat. As we pulled out of the parking lot riding low, I waved at the two smiling ladies that I was leaving behind.

We decided to eat dinner at Ruby Tuesday's across from the Orange Park Mall. I'd never been there, but all of my co-workers had been raving about it the week before so that's were I suggested that we eat. We talked for several minutes before the waitress came over to take out orders. I remember that we both ordered a well-done steak, some sides, and a tall glass of milk. Yes, I was surprised that this big Marine man ordered milk but as we now know, milk does a body good. And his was looking pretty tight that night.

After dinner, we drove over to the Orange Park Mall to pick out a movie. At that time, I was really into horror flicks and we decided to watch the newly released, *Friday the 13th*. Since we had some time to kill before the picture started, we walked through the mall holding hands and just talking about our lives and our military experiences. He'd been in the service much longer than me, so I really learned a lot from our conversation. I could tell that he was trying to move past his shyness and open up with me.

It was a scary movie which gave me a reason to hold on to him while we were in the theatre. I squeezed his hand so hard that he kept asking me, "Are you alright?"

"Yeah," I replied closing my eyes, and squeezing him tighter. The movie was so gross. I believe that I saw the whole thing through half closed eyelids. While my left hand was squeezing his right hand; my right hand was clinging to his hard muscular forearms for dear life. Finally, the movie was over and we were back in the car headed towards the base.

He asked me several times if I'd like to go get something else to eat or to drink before heading back to the base, but I politely declined. Obviously, he's wasn't quite ready for the date to end. The evening was going so well that neither one of us really wanted to say good night. With old school music playing low on the radio, we just kept driving and talking until we got tired of all that driving and all that talking.

Six months later, we were engaged to be married. I don't exactly remember the proposal, but I do remember having a discussion where we both agreed that it was "better to marry than to burn." So approximately six months after that day, we headed back to Arkansas for a June outdoor wedding. The following year, we traveled to Sicily and spent eighteen months living abroad. It was truly the best time of my life and one of the most beautiful places that we would ever visit over the next twenty-five years of marriage.

And it all started at an intersection on a central Florida Navy base because I was willing to love.

<u>About the Author</u>

Barbara Joe-Williams is an author and an independent publisher living in Tallahassee, Florida, with her husband, Wilbert, and daughter, Amani. She is the sole owner of Amani Publishing and has published three romance novels titled, *Falling for Lies, Dancing with Temptation, and Forgive Us This Day*. She's also the author of a non-fiction book titled, *One Sister's Guide to Self-Publishing: A Ten-Step Program to Success* and an E-Book titled, *A Writer's Guide to Self-Publishing & Marketing.*

Currently, she's working on another novel to be released in October titled, *A Man of My Own,* which will be her fourth book. And a marriage handbook titled, *Moving the Furniture: 52 Ways to Keep Your Marriage Fresh*, to be released in February 2008.

Ms. Williams travels as an inspirational teacher conducting seminars and workshops on writing, publishing, and marketing. She served four years in the U.S. Navy prior to attending college at Tallahassee Community College and Florida A&M University.

Blog: www.Barbarajoe.blogspot.com

Email: Amanipublishing@aol.com

Website: www.Amanipublishing.net

Coming February 2008!

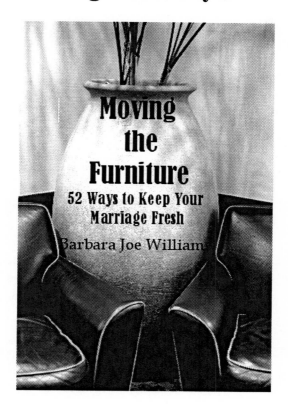

Moving the Furniture
52 Ways to Keep Your Marriage Fresh

Price: $10.00

This unique marriage handbook will give you an idea for every week of the year to keep your vows fresh. Based on over twenty-five years of marital experience, this book is a must-have for every married couple and even those that are thinking about making a lifetime commitment.

Marriage is work, but it doesn't have to be hard work.

Printed in the United States
80456LV00005BA/184-210